MURDER ON THE MOUNTAIN

A COPPER RIDGE MYSTERY - BOOK 2

AMY GRUNDY

BLUE WHISKERS
PUBLISHING

BLUE WHISKERS
PUBLISHING

ISBN - 978-1-952392-03-0

 Created with Vellum

ACKNOWLEDGMENTS

Special Thanks to:

Gracie Cassias, Beta Reader, and beautiful niece, who sent my first draft to a copy editor, despite my fears… and continued printing and shipping my manuscripts back and forth for every subsequent book, I owe her a lot of postage!

Camille Ingram, Copy Editor - Gotta love the red pen. Just kidding, but if she did use a red pen, I'd probably owe her a whole new box! No matter what color ink, her corrections made my books so much better, for that I thank her.

Sarah Hobbs, Content Editor - In just the short time we've worked together, I have learned a lot. She has the ability to cut through a clunky sentence and make it clear. Writers, if you need a content editor, you could not go wrong with Sarah.

And **Daniela Colleo**, Cover Artist - Thank you so much for your patience. I know I am very picky! If anyone needs a really Stunning Book Cover, she made it so easy for a first time author.

To my loving husband, David.
Without you this would have never happened.
You make me smile everyday.

CHAPTER ONE

EMILY

"GOOD MORNING, EMILY." I heard a familiar voice and looked around, setting down my coffee cup.

Mrs. Smithers approached my table. She was an elderly lady, with lovely white hair, impeccably applied makeup and large colorful glasses hanging around her neck. A long-time resident of Copper Ridge, Mrs. Smithers managed the town's historical society. She had previously helped me obtain information about the town and some local ghost stories too.

"Hey, good morning, Mrs. Smithers," I said, smiling. "Won't you have a seat?"

I was having breakfast at my favorite spot, The Little Copper Cafe, enjoying some sourdough French toast and crispy bacon.

"No dear, thank you though. I am just picking up a lemon poppy seed muffin before I head over to work. You know I absolutely love the muffins Claudette bakes, and if you haven't tried it, the coffee cake is scrumptious. Oh, but back to business, I wanted to ask you to stop by and see me sometime at the courthouse. I have an intriguing new story for you that I think you could use for your ghost tours." Her lively blue eyes gleamed as she smiled at me mischievously. She knew I was hooked.

"Of course. I'd love to stop by. How about after I finish up here?"

"Perfect, I'll see you soon." She turned and went to pick up her muffin from Claudette and left with a smile on her face.

Claudette, the owner of the cafe, came over and refilled my coffee cup. "Hey, how are you enjoying that French toast?" Claudette was cheery and outgoing. She was one of the first people to welcome me when I moved into town. She had soft brown hair, warm brown eyes, and just the beginnings of laugh lines around her eyes. She reminded me a lot of my mother, maybe not so much with her looks, but with her personality.

She knew I loved my carbs. "You know I never met a carb I didn't like," I laughed. "This French toast is amazing; any chance you'll give me your recipe?"

"I could, but you know if I did, you might quit coming in here to see me."

"That would never happen. Breakfast always tastes better whenever someone else cooks it for me," I laughed. "Mrs. Smithers appears to love your lemon poppy seed muffins."

"It's a new recipe, I'm glad she likes it. Seems like it's going to be popular with my customers. Speaking of which, let me get back to work and I'll leave you to get back to your breakfast before it gets cold." Claudette went on, working her way from table to table, chatting and helping her other customers. The Little Copper Cafe was quite popular in town, and for good reason.

I finished eating my breakfast, paid my check and headed out the door to see Mrs. Smithers. I couldn't help but wonder what she would have for me today.

CHAPTER TWO

EMILY

MRS. SMITHERS HAD HELPED me a several months ago when I was starting up my business of giving ghost tours here in Copper Ridge. I was excited to hear what new story she had for me. I zipped up my hoodie as the chilly autumn wind began to blow. This was my favorite time of year with the leaves of the aspen and maple trees turning vibrant shades of yellow, orange and red. I left my car at the cafe, walked across the town square and climbed the courthouse steps. Built in the 1800s, the building had limestone block walls, accented with red sandstone, capped with domes, and an intricate clock tower.

Mrs. Smithers looked up from her reading when I walked in.

"Lovely to see you, my dear." She greeted me as she closed her book. "Let me show you what I found. I think you're going to like it!"

I watched as she opened a cabinet, and pulled out a

small worn rectangular wooden box. She handed me a pair of soft white gloves, and pulled out a pair for herself as well. As I pulled my gloves on, I couldn't help but get excited. Whatever she had was obviously very old. She lifted the lid and unwrapped what looked like some sort of diary or logbook. The cover was stained, its edges battered, and she turned the old, yellowed pages very carefully.

"I found this book while looking through some information from the mine. This is a logbook that was kept by the mine manager. He kept track of many things; this one dealt with information regarding his employees. It was rather ordinary reading until I came across this section." She turned the book around and pointed.

I started reading where she indicated. "*Some of the men gave reports of witnessing lights in the woods evening last. They describe them as orbs, green or yellow in color, that appear to float, never landing on the ground. They report walking into the woods but the lights disappear and they are never able to come upon them. The men who have reported seeing these strange lights are some of my most reliable. They are not prone to drunkenness or other such indications of poor character. I am uncertain of what to make of their reports whether they are credible or folly.*"

I looked up at Mrs. Smithers. "What do you think this means?"

"Keep reading, look at this entry over here." She pointed to another page.

"*The men reported seeing the strange lights again. They say they are a sign. Others say they are a bad omen. Every time they are sighted, an accident occurs. The lights were spotted last night and today two men were injured when a support beam collapsed. Mining is far from safe work but I do not believe in the correlation. Neither myself nor my crew chief put stock in such notions. I do not want a few men spreading wild tales and causing disruption among the crew."*

"That is interesting. Do you have any information about the lights? I wonder what it was they were seeing?"

"Well, that's the interesting thing. We don't know. I suppose he wanted to keep the stories quiet. The miners themselves didn't keep journals, or if they did, we don't have any of them. After the mine closed, there was no reason for the mining camp to remain open, so it closed down. No one lived on the mountain and the story of the strange lights was forgotten. I am going to keep looking to see what else I can find out though," Mrs. Smithers said, closing the book.

"You're right, I can see why you thought this would make a good ghost story. I can use this." I stood there for a moment thinking about what she had just shown me. "Do you have a location for these supposed lights? I'd love to go up the mountain and see what I can find."

"Well I can give you a location to the old mine, but right now that's the best I can do." Mrs. Smithers pulled out a map of the mountain and the surrounding area. "Here is the old mine property," she said, marking the location. "What we don't know for certain is what direction the miners were looking in, in relation to their camp. I'll keep looking through our records here and see what else I can find. Why don't you take this map with you and if I find anything else I'll let you know. This is so exciting. I love a good mystery."

"By any chance are these the same lights people have reported seeing in the old cemetery?" I asked her.

"People around here have said those could be miners with their lamps searching for lost fellow miners. These lights could be the same, we just don't know. They've had accidents at the mine, of course, some worse than others. Sometimes a miner would make it out and later die from their injuries. Those men are the ones who are buried in the old cemetery. But then they had that big collapse, and those miner's bodies were never recovered. From what I've read, they considered closing the mine due to the lack of ore being recovered. Anyway, after the last big collapse, well that was it. They closed it down for good."

"Wow, that's quite the story. Those were some rough times. I can't imagine what it must have been like to be a miner or to live in those days. I suppose I'm way too used to my modern conveniences," I admitted.

"Yes, I suppose they were. Times have changed so much here in Copper Ridge, even since I was born."

I smiled at her, "I'll bet you have some stories to tell. Listen, I want you to know I really appreciate all the information you dig up for me. Thank you so much for taking the time to do the research and letting me know about what you find."

"Well, dear, I love researching, I've just never had anyone to share it with. You have made me feel young again."

"We make quite the pair, don't we?" I reached out and gave her a quick hug. She was such a sweet, endearing lady. "Would you care to take a drive up the mountain with me?"

"Well, I'd love to, my dear. It sounds like quite the adventure."

We scheduled our jaunt up the mountain for a day later in the week when the historical society was closed.

I watched as she wrapped the old journal and put it away. "I'd better be going. I've got errands to run today. Thanks again for the new info though. I really appreciate it."

"Oh, anytime my dear, anytime."

I left my white gloves on the counter, "Good-bye. Have a good day."

"You too, my dear."

I left the courthouse and was hit with a chilly gust of wind. I loved the mountains and I loved the fall. It just made me feel alive. I got my car and headed off to get some shopping done and couldn't help but look up at the mountain. I laughed to myself, no lights to be seen now, but of course it was daytime.

CHAPTER THREE

EMILY

I FINISHED RUNNING my errands and had plenty of time to get ready before I headed out to meet Maggie. She and I had agreed to meet for dinner that evening. Maggie, Copper Ridge's local florist was a good friend whom I had met shortly after moving to town. We were both about the same age. She had a chin-length blonde bob with lots of golden highlights, while I had long dark red hair. We met in local coffee shop, when she literally bumped into me spilling an iced latte all over my clothes. We started chatting and before I knew it, Maggie was at my house, helping me renovate my little Craftsman bungalow. We enjoyed spending time together and had hit it off right from the start. Tonight, I drove back into town to meet her at her house; it was her turn to cook. Her home was located in the top floors above her flower shop, Maggie's Creations, right off the town square. She had done a lot of the work herself, making it into an open concept downstairs and bedrooms upstairs.

She had kept the exposed brick walls, refinish the old hard-wood floors, and replaced the old glass in the arched windows. I had given her grief about living so close to her work, thinking it would be nice to get away from work and go home, but then I saw the place and knew why she loved it.

The fragrance of good home cooking met me before she even opened her door. Maggie greeted me with, "I hope you're hungry."

"Oh, my goodness, it smells wonderful in here," I said, dropping my jacket over the back of the couch.

"I made us some good old-fashioned comfort food tonight. When the weather turns chilly, I like to indulge myself. How does homemade chicken pot pie sound?"

"It sounds absolutely wonderful, and look at that crust." My mouth watered as I looked at the golden flaky crust. We served our plates and sat down to eat. Things had started to quiet down in town following the murder of our town's lead newspaper reporter, Simon Wilson. Copper Ridge was a small town of approximately eight thousand or so and was situated at the base of Angel Mountain. The town had most recently re-invented itself and made most of its income from tourism. We had mountains in the area for hiking and camping, a river running through town for rafting, along with a fair number of artisans and craftsmen who had come to town, opening shops mostly around the old town square. I was a recent newcomer to town myself following the death of my mother. She had left me with a modest inheritance and I had started a business giving ghost tours. The town was full of old historic sites which I used as stops on my tour.

"Maggie, this is so good. You'll have to show me how to

make a crust like this," I laughed. "Or better yet, I'll just let you cook dinner for me more often."

"Not on your life," She laughed.

"So, what's new?" I asked, sipping my coffee.

"By any chance do you want to make a trip up the mountain with me, maybe this weekend?" Maggie asked

"Sure." I looked up, curious that the mountain had come up twice in conversations now. "But why are we going up there?" Besides the old abandoned mine, most of the mountain was heavily wooded and not very developed. There were some private cabins dotted about for seasonal guests and rough hiking trails, some streams for fishing, but not much else.

"Several years ago, an elderly gentleman came into the shop. Seems his wife was dying and he had me order multiple kinds of orchids for delivery to their home, some quite exotic. He lived in a gated estate about thirty miles from here. It wasn't a huge house, but he did have a good bit of property, with some lovely gardens from what I saw. Anyway, seemed like orchids were her favorite. So, for the last weeks of her life, he surrounded her with them. He had us making trips to their home several times a week, bringing in more and more of them. He loved her so much." Maggie's voice got a little quieter. "Then she died." From the look on her face I knew she was remembering her customer during that tragic time. "He was so sad and very distraught. He gave me very specific instructions regarding the kind of flowers he wanted for her funeral. I made sure they were perfect, and just what he wanted. He was such a sweet old guy. Anyway, after the funeral, I didn't see or hear from him anymore. Recently though, his attorney stopped by the shop. Seems like the old gentleman has also now passed away and he left me some land up on the mountain. I thought I'd go up there and take a look."

"Wow. Those must have been some special flowers."

"I think he was lonely and so appreciative of the care and attention we showed him and his wife. I tried my best to be as exact as possible, always getting specifically what he wanted."

"You were what he needed, at a time when he needed it the most."

"Well, I was just glad to be able to be there for him, even if it was just to deliver the flowers. I would never have expected anything in return, much less have something left to me in a will." Maggie replied.

"Well, let's go check it out. I really wanted to go up there anyway. Mrs. Smithers and I were talking this morning. It seems like back when the mine was open, there were reports of some of the miners seeing unexplained lights off in the woods. The miners tried to follow the lights through the forest, but the lights would just vanish. The information Mrs. Smither's showed me said the miners thought the lights were a bad omen. So, she and I plan to drive up the mountain to the old mine and have a look around."

"It's settled then. Why don't you let her know what time to meet and we'll go see my property and look for those lights." Maggie glanced over at my empty plate. "Want some more?"

"No, I'm good. That was really delicious." Maggie took my plate and walked off to the kitchen. "Promise me, you'll make that again sometime."

Are you ready for dessert?" She called out from the kitchen.

"Dessert? Maybe you should have said there would be dessert; I might have stopped eating sooner."

"Oh, don't give me that, you know you have room for dessert." Maggie knew I'd probably have to be dying to pass up a dessert.

And then she brought it to the table. Lava brownies baked in little iron skillets and now topped with vanilla ice cream and extra hot fudge. "Ta-da!"

I cut into that chocolate brownie and the warm, rich, creamy chocolate center oozed out, mixing with my melting ice cream. "Oh, I think I've died and gone to chocolate heaven."

We chatted more and before you knew it, we were both scraping the chocolate remains from our dishes. "I think I'm going to explode, but what a way to go."

We washed the dishes together, then firmed up our plans for the weekend.

"Thanks for dinner, next time it'll be my turn to cook," I promised. See you this weekend."

As I made my way downstairs to my car, I couldn't help but glance up at the mountain. Of course, I didn't see any dots of light up there now, all was dark. I couldn't help but wonder how many cabins were up there and if anyone up there had ever seen lights or anything else out of the ordinary. What had the miners actually seen?

CHAPTER FOUR

EMILY

I MET Mrs. Smithers on Saturday morning at The Little Copper Cafe. I was always impressed by her impeccable makeup and hair style. I loved her red lipstick but didn't think I could pull off that color with my red hair. We planned to get a bite to eat before taking our drive up the mountain.

"So, are you going to get a lemon poppy seed muffin or try something else?" I asked her.

"Oh, today, let's see," she said while she was poring over the menu. "Oh, I think I'll try the cinnamon roll and a cup of coffee. How about you, my dear?"

"I think I might try one of those lemon poppy seed muffins after all. Maybe with a side of fruit, then at least my breakfast will be somewhat healthier," I laughed. "Oh, and if you don't mind, we're also going to meet Maggie here in a bit. She's going to be going up the mountain with us."

"Of course, my dear. The more the merrier, I say."

About that time, I heard Claudette call out, "Good morning, Maggie."

I looked up and waved Maggie over to our table.

"Good morning, ladies, I hope I didn't keep you," she said, pulling out a chair.

"Hey, Maggie! No, we were just getting ready to order." I replied as I handed her a menu.

Claudette came over and poured coffee for all of us. "What would you ladies like for breakfast today?"

"I'd love to try one of your cinnamon rolls," Mrs. Smithers said. "They just look so decadent with all that gooey icing."

Claudette turned to me. "I'll take a bowl of fruit, and I'd love to try one of your lemon poppy seed muffins."

"You're going to love it." Claudette laughed, "They are quite good, even if I do say so myself. And how about you, Maggie, what can I get for you?"

"How about a blueberry bagel and cream cheese? I'm good with that."

"I'll get this started for you, ladies, and will be right back."

"This is so exciting," Mrs. Smithers said, clapping her hands together. "I love a good adventure. So, Maggie are you going to help us track down some mysterious lights up on the mountain?"

"I sure am. Whatever you need and then we can check out some property up there."

"I want to thank you ladies for bringing me along," Mrs. Smithers was beaming with excitement. "I don't get to have too many adventures these days."

In just a few minutes, breakfast arrived. Maggie and I

glanced at Mrs. Smithers' plate and then each other. We busted out laughing. Mrs. Smithers looked at her plate, "Oh my, is this one cinnamon roll? It's huge! I think I might need a to-go box."

We enjoyed our breakfast together and I made myself a mental note to come back some time to get one of those cinnamon rolls. It didn't bother me that it was practically the size of a dinner plate.

"So, Maggie, what sort of property do you have up there?" Mrs. Smithers asked.

"Well, I haven't seen it yet, but I think there are some summer cabins up there. I don't think the previous owner had many active renters for the last several years though. I need to see what it's like up there, check out the cabins and see what sort of shape they're in. If I'm lucky maybe there will be a possibility of renting them out in the summer."

"It really would be awesome if you can fix them up for summer rentals. Cabins up on the mountain could bring more tourists into town. That would help all of our businesses, including my ghost tour business." I responded.

"And just think, my dear, if we actually find those ghost lights up on the mountain, that could give you a new stop on your tour," Mrs. Smithers said.

Maggie laughed, "As long as those lights don't scare away my renters. For now, it's one step at a time for me."

"If anyone can make it work, it would be you, Maggie." I glanced about the cafe, "And speaking of work, it looks like Claudette is doing a pretty good business here today. I'll bet she is going to have to hire some additional help soon." The cafe was full and there were many faces there that I did not recognize, including the couple sitting at the table next to ours. The weather was turning cooler and the rafting company had closed down for the season, but we still had people coming into town. Maybe some were here doing some early Christmas shopping.

We finished eating, paid our bill, and waved goodbye to Claudette as we headed out.

CHAPTER FIVE

EMILY

WE LEFT THE CAFE, excited to see what the day would hold. Mrs. Smithers made sure we had our map that would direct us to the location of the old mine and camp. Maggie had directions to her new property and the multiple cabins. It was one of those days with vivid blue skies and just the right temperature, not too hot and not too cold. It was the perfect day for our little field trip.

Eventually, we turned off the main road heading out of town and pointed the car in the direction of the mountain. The two-lane road was bordered by the oaks, aspens and pines. The leaves were so pretty up here. Occasionally, there were gaps in the trees and we could get a glimpse of the hills and valleys below. It was an incredible view and I loved this part of the country. Pretty soon we found our turnoff and headed toward some of the property that Maggie now owned.

It turned out she had been a little less forthcoming on

what was now hers. She actually owned approximately a hundred acres of the mountain. Almost all of it was heavily wooded. She also had five cabins, three of which, according to the map appeared to be on the western edge of a mountain lake. We took the road that would lead us up to the lake. Two of the cabins were next door to each other and then the other was set off by itself farther down the same road.

"Well, what do you know, lakefront property," I said excitedly. We were all oohing and aahing as we drove up. We were more impressed by the views than anything. "I haven't been up the mountain since I moved here. I had no idea there was a lake up here." I was looking around almost speechless.

"My husband and I used to come up here for picnics when we were courting," Mrs. Smithers said with a dreamy look on her face. "There were no homes up here at that time. We were so young then. When the babies came along, we didn't come up here as often, but when we did, we had such fun times, swimming and fishing. The children are all grown up and have gotten on with their own lives and, well, I never thought I'd ever get back up here again."

Maggie turned gave her a quick hug, and said, "Well, we'll have to see what we can do about getting you back up here more often, especially if I can get these cabins fixed up."

The lakeside cabins were a good size, all of which had big decks overlooking the lake, although they were in sad shape. "These cabins are definitely in need of repair," Maggie said, looking around. "Some of this I think I might be able to manage on my own, but I'm definitely out of my league when it comes to putting on a new roof." Maggie looked around, her eyes twinkling and a look of excitement on her face.

Home improvement was not my forte, and I know she saw my look of skepticism.

"I said I'd need some help," she said.

"I think they could make some awesome rental properties, at least, if you can make them rentable." I wasn't sure if Maggie even heard me. I could see the wheels in her head turning. She was envisioning the potential. She was good at that. We hopped back in the car and drove a little bit farther up the mountain.

"There it is," Mrs. Smithers called out. "That should be the turnoff to the mine."

We drove down a bumpy rut filled road for about five minutes. The trees weren't quite as thick up here, but the underbrush was creeping in on both sides of the narrow dirt road. The car was slowly bumping along and then we had to stop altogether. There was a chain across the road with a posted sign.

"Well, I guess this is as far as we can go," I sighed. "Bummer." I really wanted to get as close to the mine as possible.

"Come on, dearie, where's your sense of adventure?"

I turned in my seat, looking back at Mrs. Smithers, in time to see her climbing out of the car. Maggie and I hurried to catch up with her.

"Mrs. Smithers, where are you going? You can't go through there," Maggie said.

We watched Mrs. Smithers nimbly duck under the chain that blocked the path, and start off down the dirt road on the other side.

Maggie turned to look at me, "Well, I guess she can."

· · ·

"HEY, WAIT FOR US," I called after her. We were being left behind.

"Well, come on, hurry up, my dears. Don't keep an old lady waiting."

We reached the mine and started to look around, steering clear of the actual mine entrance, which was boarded up and gated off.

"Wow, look at those views." Mrs. Smithers drew our attention, "We're quite a ways up here, aren't we?"

"Be careful, and let's not get too close to the edge." My heart beat a little faster as I took a few steps away from the edge. Hopefully my fear of heights was not too obvious.

"So, with the mountain behind us, the ghost lights could be in these three directions," Mrs. Smithers said, pointing.

Looking out, all we could see was forest, a little bit of a river, and down and off to one side we could see a little portion of the lake.

"Look, Maggie, if that's the lake, I wonder where your cabins are?" I asked, pointing in the direction of the lake.

"I don't know, I sure don't see them down there, but there isn't much of the lake showing. And speaking of which, you ladies do know you probably wouldn't see any little floating orbs of light in the daytime, right?" Maggie was giving us a look like we were nuts.

"Well, I know that. But we wanted to see where the mine was in relation to the town below, and get a feel for what it's like up here." Actually, a little of the old city could be seen from the mine, but most of it was off to one side and wasn't visible due to the forest. "Isn't that right, Mrs. Smithers?"

"That's right, my dears. Now what you need to do is come back after dark and see if the orbs of light appear."

"After dark?" Maggie yelped, "Why, it would be pitch

black up here. There aren't any street lights or anything. How would you even begin to manage?"

"Well, my dear, with help from you of course. Now you know where you are going and which road to turn on, it'll be easier to find. Surely, you can't expect Emily to come up here and tromp around through the woods by herself. There is no telling what sort of animals or things could be up here."

I gave Maggie my best pitiful look. "Yes, you wouldn't want me to be up here all by myself."

Maggie threw up her hands, "Oh, I give up. Okay, I'll come back up here with you." She turned around, shaking her head and mumbling, "I can't believe you want to be up here in the dark."

I gave a smile and a thumbs-up to Mrs. Smithers behind Maggie's back. She smiled back with a devious little gleam in her eyes. We all climbed back in the car and headed just a little farther up the mountain. The roads seemed to become even more narrow than before, and the turns a little tighter, if that was even possible.

"We should be getting closer," I said, peering at the map.

"I think we are here," Maggie pointed to a cabin we were approaching. She stopped the car at the first cabin and got out to have a look around. "Watch your step, Mrs. Smithers, this ground is a little uneven," Maggie advised.

"I will indeed," she responded.

I turned slowly in a circle looking around. "This is actually a beautiful property, Maggie. Or it was at one time. It's terribly overgrown, but that's nothing that some hard work won't remedy." It had an awe-inspiring view down onto the valley below.

Maggie had walked up onto the wide porch and

unlocked the door. "Watch the steps, some of these boards are almost rotted through."

"I'll just wait right here," Mrs. Smithers responded.

I walked up the steps gingerly and entered the cabin. The power was off, of course, and the inside was dark, but we could both tell it had potential.

"Maggie, this is a good space; it obviously needs some fixing up, but just like the cabins by the lake, overall they're not in that bad of shape. Get them fixed up and they'll make some great rental properties."

"I wonder how much it will take to get them repaired?" she asked, "I need to hire someone to inspect all of the cabins and give me an estimate."

"Well, I'm here for you, and I can roll up my sleeves to pitch in, especially since you taught me a thing or two about home remodeling."

"So, girls, how did it look inside?" Mrs. Smithers asked as we stepped back onto the porch. "This is such a lovely spot up here, so quiet and peaceful."

"Well, I think Maggie has a diamond in the rough. It just needs some polishing up." We stopped at the last cabin and found it in similar shape. Yards, if you could call them that, were more than a bit overgrown, and the steps, porches and decks were in desperate need of repair. At least one of the cabins looked like it could use a new roof. And all of them could obviously use updates to the interiors.

"You know, dear, you could start slow on these. Get one or two fixed up and rented and then that will give you income to start in on the others," Mrs. Smithers noted.

"Yes, and I may just have to do that. I'm really glad we came up here today to at least get a look at them. Thanks, ladies, for coming along with me. Why don't we head back to town and have some lunch?"

"You dears have given me such a treat today, I have so enjoyed getting out of the house and coming back up here."

"We've loved having you along," I said, giving her a big smile. She was such a little dear, and so lively for her age.

"Please keep me updated, if you don't mind. I'd love to know if you ever spot any strange floating lights."

"We certainly will," I laughed to myself as I noticed the hesitant look on Maggie's face. She was definitely not the adventurous type.

CHAPTER SIX

RENEE

I WOKE up with a start and looked out the window. We were still driving. My heart sank when I realized we were still on the road. There were dark clouds forming in the sky, and we appeared to be driving up a mountain. I sighed, not knowing how I had allowed Michael to talk me into this situation. "Where are we?" I looked over at Michael. He still had a serious look on his face, his brown hair a ruffled mess.

"Almost there," was all he said.

"But where is there?" Michael had been very vague with the details.

"I used to come up here with my parents when I was a kid," Michael started to explain. "There were a few cabins on this mountain. They were pretty isolated and most people don't even know they are up here. We should be safe for now."

I sighed and looked back out the car window. "You

know I had a good job at the new salon. I was just starting to build up my clientele again, and now I've up and walked away from it."

"We won't be up here too long. Just until the investigation is more established, or maybe until they make some arrests. Then we can return home and you can go back to work. Look, Renee, I'm just trying to keep us safe."

"What was the latest you heard from the prosecutor? How long do you think this is going to take?"

"I think they should be serving the warrants soon. Then they'll be able to go through the company records and find the proof they need to make the arrests. You know, I always thought Prism Chemical was a fairly good company to work for. I thought they were doing good research. Who knew they could be so irresponsible and would ever take any part in anything illegal, much less dumping toxic waste?"

"I wish you had never read that email. Couldn't you have just left it alone and not been snooping about in the first place?" My voice was rising and I felt the knots of tension in my shoulders.

"Renee, I know you don't mean that." Michael paused, looking over at me, "and I wasn't exactly snooping either. You know how much I wanted that promotion. I was just trying to be better informed.

"You didn't need that promotion. We were doing just fine the way we were. Now you've got us tangled up in this mess, because you were greedy."

"It doesn't matter what my motives were, I just know there are things that can't be unheard and can't be unseen. Prism can't get away with just dumping their toxic waste wherever they want."

"I know, I know, but now they are trying to make us part

of their toxic waste dump. I don't like the feeling of being chased by someone or having someone wanting to kill me."

"And you think I do?" Michael's voice was getting higher pitched. "I just wanted to go to work, do my job and maybe get a little ahead. I wasn't looking for trouble. And I'll do everything I can to keep us safe. No one will know we're up here. We can hide out and they'll never find us. I'll go into town periodically and use a pay phone to call the prosecutor and get us news on what's going on."

I snorted, "If you can find a pay phone."

"Renee, stop it! I'm doing the best I can. Cut me some slack already."

Michael slowed the car and turned it down a small road. It had a lot of overgrowth along the side of the road. I hoped it was as deserted up here as he remembered it. Michael brought the car to a stop as we neared a run-down cabin set way back off the road. We both got out of the car and slowly approached the house.

"Michael, how do you know no one is living here?"

He might not have meant to, but I saw the scowl on his face. "Does it look like anyone is living here? Wait here. I'll be right back."

He walked off, edging quietly up to the cabin. He disappeared around the back corner and circled the whole cabin. As he came back from the other side he looked in one of the windows. He waved for me, it was all clear.

"Now what? Are we going to break in?"

He bent down and moved a rock on the corner of the back porch. He took a key from underneath the rock and unlocked the door. "How did you know that was there?" I asked hesitantly.

"That's where it was when I was a kid. Like I said, I

came up with my parents for several summers. It was always there."

"Hmm." I followed him into the cabin.

He flipped the light switch, but nothing happened.

"Great, an old dilapidated cabin and no power." I sighed in frustration.

"That's a good thing. Just shows us that no one lives here and by the look of it no one's been here in quite a while." Michael went back to retrieve the car. It wasn't easy, but he was able to drive the car around to the back of the cabin, trying to block it from being seen from the road. "Let's get our stuff in."

Michael had made sure we had camping gear and all the necessities to keep us fed and sheltered for a while, in case the cabin wasn't available. We had some food and water, but whether he liked it or not, we'd have to make a trip into town at some point for more groceries. I flung apart the old moth-eaten curtains, sending dust flying.

"Not those," he said sharply. "Leave the curtains facing the road closed."

"Are you kidding me? You just said it didn't look like anyone's been up here lately."

"And we don't want to make it look like anyone's here either." Michael held his hands out, "Look, I'm just trying to do what I can to keep us safe."

I pressed my lips together, knowing it was no use to argue. I turned and flung them closed, sending even more dust spiraling through the air. I managed to find an old broom and began to try to make the cabin livable. This was going to be interesting.

CHAPTER SEVEN

EMILY

I CONTINUED my business giving ghost tours several nights during the week. We had stops in town starting from the old Gage Hotel. As the story goes, the unfortunate Mr. Gage was killed in an untimely accident. He is said to be haunting his own hotel, searching for his bride. We would also walk through the town square and around the court-house. It was built in the late 1800s. Limestone walls accented by red sandstone are capped by mansard-style domes. Its most striking feature was the intricate clock tower. The old jail was the next stop on our tour. It was a very small two-story square building with very thick lime-stone walls. There were still bars on rectangular windows on the ground floor. The upper floor was said to have housed the prison guard and his family. At this time, I didn't have access to the interior of the building, but some people in town have said they could occasionally hear what sounded like the clanking of shackles. The other stops on the tour included Evergreen Manor, The Carriage House and the old Copper Ridge Cemetery.

Since hearing the tales of reported lights up on the mountain, I had begun reading up on ghost lights or orbs of lights seen in other parts of the country. I wanted to see if there were logical explanations or causes for this phenomenon. Seems like some ghost lights could be attributed to different things like swamp gas, or lights caused by atmospheric phenomena. There is some speculation about various minerals interacting and causing lights, the old legends like the will o' wisp, and some stories of lights that have no explanation at all. I knew that I was going to have to go up on the mountain and see if I could see them.

Although Maggie had said she would go back up there with me at night, I knew it was something she really didn't want to do. Even if we did go back up there together, she wouldn't want to stay long, much less wander around in the forest at night by ourselves. I was pretty certain she was born without the adventure gene. Maybe I could bribe her with chocolate or a lifetime supply of baked goods from The Little Copper Cafe. Claudette, who owned the little cafe, was an awesome baker. I closed my laptop and hopped up. Time to pay a visit to my pal.

I made my way into town, it was overcast out, but wasn't due to rain until later that night. For now, I thought I'd be safe to walk. I opened the door to the cafe and saw Claudette wiping down the countertop.

"Hey, Claudette. How are you doing?"

"Hey. You just caught me. I'm getting ready to close up for the day. You're a little late for lunch."

"Oh, no. I just came in to see if you had any muffins or scones left. And I'll take it to go, if you have anything."

"Yes, I have some of the orange cranberry bread, and brown sugar cinnamon scones."

My eyes, lite up and I thought to myself, it didn't take much to make me happy. "Sounds good. I'll take two of each if you have that, thanks."

"Sure, I'll get them and be right back." Claudette went off to get my order and came back shortly with four small bags. I placed them gently in my little canvas tote bag, and paid for my treats.

"Thanks, Claudette, you're the best."

"You have a good day sweetie, I'll see you later." She gave me a wave good-bye as I left.

Part one of my mission was accomplished. Now for part two. My next stop was at the coffee shop. I ordered two large hot caramel lattes. This was Maggie's favorite and I loved them too, but then again, I loved all of them, hot cold, caramel, vanilla. So far, I hadn't met a latte that I didn't like.

I entered the flower shop, looking around for Maggie. Kelly, Maggie's part-time employee was manning the desk. "Hello, is Maggie here?"

"No, she said she had to run an errand."

My shoulders sagged. So, I was standing there with two lattes in hand and no one to bribe. "Any idea when she'll be back?"

"No, I'm sorry, she didn't say."

"Well isn't that special." I stood there holding the two sugary lattes and wondering what to do now.

"What's special?" I jumped and turned.

"Hey, Maggie," I said, holding out the coffee.

"You read my mind. Thanks, I was wanting one of those, but didn't want to be gone too long from the shop. Thanks, Kelly, for minding the store. You can go ahead and go now."

"Thanks, Maggie." Kelly gathered up her books and left.

"How's Kelly working out for you?"

"She's good. She's a senior at the high school, very responsible and is working out well for when I need just a little extra help. She's doesn't have the knowledge Priscilla had about plants and arrangements, but we know how that turned out." Priscilla had swept into town and ended up killing Simon, the lead reporter of our town's newspaper. He was also Priscilla's half-brother. She killed Simon for his share of the family inheritance. Priscilla had held us at gunpoint until the police swarmed Maggie's shop. We had barely escaped with our lives.

"Well, I'm glad she's no Priscilla. Being confronted by a killer is not my idea of a good afternoon. Oh, here, I brought you something else." I reached into my bag and pulled out the orange cranberry bread and a brown sugar cinnamon scone. "Thought you might like an afternoon pick-me-up."

"Oh wow. What did I do to deserve this? I love everything Claudette makes, thanks. Come on back here to the back and pull up a stool and we can visit."

I followed her to the back and took a seat at one of her work counters. "Why, can't I be a good friend and bring you a treat for no reason?" I laughed, trying not to sound guilty.

"Did you want one of these?" she asked, holding out the little pastry bags to me.

"No, those are yours, this one is mine," I said, pulling the other scone out of my bag. "These are so good," I said, savoring my first bite. "So, I started reading about the ghost lights; seems like there is a lot of speculation. Theories are all over the place. Everything from swamp gas to will o' wisps. I want to go back up there at night and see what I can see."

"Well, as long as you don't ask me to come along," Maggie paused and then looked up all of a sudden. "That's why you're here. Is this your idea of a bribe? You want me to go up there with you. Nope, not doing it!" She said shaking her head. She continued to eat her scone.

"Ah, Maggie, come on. Please, you don't want me going up there all by myself," I said, sounding pathetic.

"You are such a little weasel," she said, laughing. "You know I don't really want to go up there in the dark, but still, you don't have to bribe me."

"Oh, well, then give me back the orange cranberry bread then."

"Never," she laughed moving the bag out of my reach.

"Thank you, Maggie," my voice sounding extra sweet.

"Uh-huh, whatever," she said, continuing to enjoy her scone.

I was relieved to know I wouldn't have to sit on some mountainside in the dark by myself. Nothing like having your partner in crime watch ghostly lights with you!

CHAPTER EIGHT

CLAUDETTE

"I'LL HAVE THE PANCAKES, bacon and coffee. Thank you." The young man sat at one of the front tables by the window. He had sandy blonde hair and a muscular build.

"Coming right up," I said. I turned in his order and began making my rounds with the coffee pot. Even though summer was over, we were still getting a lot of tourists in town. I'd never complain about being busy, after all it was good for business. I approached another table toward the back of the cafe and walked by, hearing part of a conversation.

"We should never have come here," the man said. "I don't know how I let you talk me into this."

"Don't worry, Michael, you worry too much. We're going to be fine. There is no one here from your company," the lady with him responded.

"More coffee for either of you?" Claudette asked.

"Yes, please," the lady responded, holding up her cup. "That breakfast was the best I've had in a while now."

"Well then, you'll have to come back soon for another. We have quite good lunches too," I said. I loved having satisfied customers.

"Don't think we'll be doing that," the man said rather curtly.

I smiled at the man, not taking any offense. I thought I heard the lady call him Michael and I presumed they were just passing through. "Well, if you ever come this way again, feel free to stop by." I moved on, going to the service window to pick up an order. I picked up the stack of pancakes and bacon and brought it back to the man sitting by the window.

"Oh, this looks so good." The pancakes were fluffy-looking with a puddle of butter in the middle.

"I'll bring you more coffee." I took a quick scan of the little cafe and went back to pick up the coffee pot. I returned to his table to make sure everything was okay and refilled his coffee cup.

"I haven't had pancakes this good since I was a kid. My mother was an awesome cook and these are almost as good as hers."

"Almost?" I laughed, "Well, I suppose I will take an almost. You enjoy those and I'll come back and check on you in a bit."

I made my way from table to table, with the coffee pot, eventually making it to the back to the couple's table. "Well, you both have cleaned your plates. Could I get you anything else or would you like some scones or muffins to go?"

"Yes, please, how about four of your blueberry muffins and two slices of the orange cranberry bread and two brown sugar cinnamon scones," the lady smiled, placing her order.

"I'll get those boxed up for you now." I turned to go, but saw a brief look that the man gave the lady.

I turned to the table behind them to refill the coffee cups of other customers. I took my time, trying to pour the coffee as slowly as possible. It paid off.

"Look, you practically forced me to come along with you. We have limited food up there in that dilapidated cabin."

"Would you keep your voice down?" the man responded to her sharply.

That was all I heard, there was only so long I could take to fill a coffee cup. I walked back to box up the pastries that the couple ordered. A few moments later they met me at the counter, picked up their pastries, paid their bill and left. What they didn't know is while they were paying their check, the man sitting by the window was watching them closely. Later on, I made my way past his table again, to gather up his dishes.

"So, what is there to do in your fair little town?"

"Well, we might be small, but we have fun. Rafting in the summer, shopping year-round. There is quite a selection of shops around the square here, everything from jewelry to a handcrafted toy shop, lots of artists, and a few galleries. Given the opportunity, I would always promote the other businesses in town. We also have hiking up on the mountain. I heard recently there were some cabins up on the mountain, but they still need some work. Maybe by next summer they will be ready to rent. Oh, and there is also a ghost tour several nights a week. They meet at the old Gage Hotel, you should go check it out."

"Hmm, so maybe there is more going on here than I thought. A ghost tour, huh, might be fun. I guess a lot of your tourists take the tour."

"I don't know about a lot, but I like to plug the local businesses when I can. A friend of mine runs it. Guess I'm just trying to help her out a bit."

"Well, maybe I can give it a shot."

CHAPTER NINE

EMILY

AFTER BREAKFAST, I decided it was finally time to make a run by the grocery store. I didn't like shopping, so I tried to be as thorough as possible, taking my time walking the aisles. Small towns are not known for their massive grocery stores and Copper Ridge was no exception. I had my cart at one end of the aisle scanning the flavored coffees and I couldn't help but overhear a conversation coming from a couple on the next aisle over.

"Come on, Renee, hurry up. Canned beans are canned beans; who cares what brand we get?"

"I'm looking to see what other canned goods we can get. I can't eat beans every day."

"Just hurry it up," the man complained. "We don't want anyone to see us."

"Listen here, I didn't want to be here with you. I was perfectly content at home, but no, you drug me up here, so you can just deal."

I heard them heading my way and I quickly wheeled my shopping cart to the next aisle over. I sure didn't want them to think I had been listening, but it was hard to ignore a conversation like they were having. I continued my shopping and found myself in a similar situation a couple of aisles over. Their conversation hadn't gotten any more civil.

"If you don't hurry up, I'm just going to leave," The man was saying in a rather unpleasant tone.

"Go then. I can troop back up to that shack all by myself. I don't know what your problem is. Just give me another minute."

If I had thought their conversation was heated before, it had risen to all out spiteful. I had heard enough. I turned and wheeled my cart to the checkout. If I missed anything I could come back. I checked out and loaded up the bags in my car. As I shut the back hatch, I looked up, and noticed the couple climbing into a car not too far away from me. They appeared to be out of words for each other, but I couldn't help but notice the daggers they were shooting in each other's direction. I sat there, remembering a previously failed relationship that I had been in. It made me sad, making that trip down memory lane, and wondering what could have been. I had been in a relationship prior to moving to Copper Ridge, but when my mother fell ill, it showed a side of him that I was not willing to put up with. I sure hoped that couple would be able to work out their differences.

CHAPTER TEN

ADAM

I DROVE INTO TOWN, wondering who would ever want to live in this little backwater place? It didn't make sense, if you're on the run and going to go into hiding, why would you hide in a small town? Why not a big city?

I drove around the town square, past some of the local hotels and even out to the hotels right off the interstate. My information said the man I was tracking had come to Copper Ridge. So far, I hadn't seen his car anywhere. Unfortunately for me, my employer was getting anxious wanting to know where the man was. Michael Jameson was his name. Seems like he was a trouble maker. He reportedly broke into some electronic files at work, read some emails he shouldn't have, threatened to blackmail his company and now it seemed like he was just going to blow the whistle on the whole thing. I had been hired on the side to take care of the situation quietly. I understood my orders. First step was to find him. I sighed heavily, I had enough of this car. I

circled the square and pulled my SUV into a parking spot
in the town square. I walked down the street the air was still
and the sky was grey and overcast. I watched a few people
crossing the square, but none that looked like my target. I
think it was time for a break. I entered The Three Pines
Bistro and Tavern. It was a nice enough looking place with
an open beam ceiling, hardwood floors. It had an open parti-
tion dividing what looked like the bar side from the restaurant side. I pulled up a seat at the bar and ordered a beer. I
had taken a quick glance around when I first came in, but
the mirror over the back of the bar gave me a good view of
the diners seated behind me. I caught site of my reflection as
well and noticed the residual scar on my cheek from a prior
job. Guess that was just an occupational hazard. The bar
tender walked back by. Maybe he'd be good for some
information.

"So, this is quite the town you have here. What do
people like to do for fun?"

"The rafting is great, but it's shut down for the season.
We have a few hiking trails up on the mountain. Around
here it's mostly the shopping that brings people to town.
Oh, and the ghost tour, if you are into that sort of thing.
Honestly, this is a pretty small quiet town. If you're looking
for night life, you're not going to find it here."

"Well, maybe I can check out that tour or maybe head
up the mountain to see what I can find."

The bartender paused looking at his watch, "If you're
really serious about that tour, it'll start in about an hour over
at the Gage Hotel."

"Thanks."

I finished up my beer and left in plenty of time to find
the hotel. I wasn't sure it would be interesting, but that
wasn't the point. I had a job to do and who knows where

this guy could be. Maybe I'd get lucky and Michael would show up for the tour or maybe I'd find some information that would point me in the right direction. I knew how to pour on the charm when I needed to. So, I figured I'd take the tour and see what information I could discover.

CHAPTER ELEVEN

EMILY

I STOOD outside the Gage Hotel waiting for my clients for tonight's ghost tour. I had five people booked, two couples and one other man. It was a cool night with a bit of a breeze which had started to pick up. I knew when it actually turned cold my tour season would be over. I was working on arrangements with the owners of the B&B about offering a special Christmas tour and party. It was a work in progress, but for tonight I was giving my tour.

"Hello, is this the ghost tour?" I watched the man approach me. He had short dark hair, dark eyes and a stylish three-day beard. It was hard to miss the scar on his exposed cheek.

"Yes, it is. I'm Emily"

"I'm Adam." He smiled and reached out to shake my hand. "I'm sorry I didn't call ahead or make any sort of reservation. I hope that's not going to be a problem."

"No, not at all. I only have a few people scheduled for

tonight. Are you in town for vacation?" I asked while collecting his payment.

"Something like that. Do you get a lot of tourists here?"

"Yes, Copper Ridge is pretty small, and it's mostly a tourist town."

Another man and a couple walked up about that time and introductions were made.

"We have one other couple scheduled to join us tonight. We'll give them a few more minutes and see if they show up." We waited another ten minutes past the time the tour would start, and then I decided to start the tour. I hated starting without everyone there, but it would take us about fifteen minutes or so to get through the hotel anyway. That would give them a little more time to arrive.

We finished up at the hotel and the other couple still had not shown up, so I continued the tour walking my guests across the town plaza. We had an uneventful tour and ended up back at the hotel. The couple thanked me, said good night and walked back inside. Adam had also thanked me and walked off, leaving me standing there with a man named Steven.

"I enjoyed the tour. I'm new in town and your tour was recommended to me," he said, shaking my hand. He was an average height, but muscular with sandy blonde hair.

"Thanks, I appreciate that. So, who recommended the tour?" I asked.

"The lady over at the, what is it, The Little Copper Cafe down the street. I was in there this morning for break-fast, which was really good by the way."

"Oh, you must mean Claudette. Yes, she is very supportive of my business. What brings you to Copper Ridge, if you don't mind me asking?"

"I'm in construction, but like I said, I'm new to the area

and I'm looking around. The lady at the cafe mentioned something about some cabins up on the mountain that needed repair. I'll have to go back over there and see if she knows who owns them. I was wondering if the owner needs any help with them."

Well, news of those cabins certainly does get around, I thought to myself. "I can ask around if you like. Are you staying here at the Gage Hotel?"

"No, it's definitely out of my league. Here's my card; if you hear anything about the cabins, please give me a call."

"I sure will, thank you." His card had a construction logo on it. But, I was getting a vibe off of him that I just didn't like. Maybe I was just being overly paranoid. My job was to meet strangers on every tour; I couldn't afford to get spooked.

"Hey, Maggie," I called her when I got home. "So, I had this guy named Steven on my tour tonight. He works in construction and he was asking about the possibility of working on the cabins."

"Well, I haven't quite got that far yet. I'm needing to get my finances in order and get them inspected. Any idea how he found out about the work?"

"Yeah, he was in the cafe and Claudette mentioned it. I don't know exactly what she told him though. I didn't give him any specifics on the number of cabins or the possible extent of the work. I have his card. I can always bring it by sometime and you can follow up with him."

"That sounds good. I have an appointment day after tomorrow with the inspector. We'll see what shape the cabins are in and then I can figure out a plan. I'm thinking I want to start on the ones by the lake first. I think they have the most rental potential."

"I think you are right, especially since they are lakeside. Let me know how it all turns out with the inspector."

"Of course."

"Want to do dinner after the inspection? You can let me know what they discovered. I can cook, it's my turn after all."

"Sounds like a plan. And, by the way, don't forget dessert."

I laughed, "Do I ever?"

CHAPTER TWELVE

STEVEN

I TURNED my truck and made my way up the mountain. I thought since I had the time, why not take a drive up there and see what I could see? I hadn't heard back from anyone about that possible construction job as of yet. The roads were quite twisty and I could see there wasn't much up there, just a lot of nothing.

I turned down another road and found the lake. There were a few cabins there, but they all looked deserted. I wondered if these were some that the lady from the cafe talked about. They definitely looked like they could use some repairs. I got back in my truck and drove farther up the mountain to see what else I could see. It didn't take too long before I found a couple of other cabins. I didn't stop to inspect them. One of the cabins looked like it might be occupied. I found another side road, parked my truck, got out and doubled back through the woods. Sure enough, there was a late-model car parked behind one of the cabins.

There was a man out back chopping wood and a thin wisp of smoke curling out of the chimney. I watched as a lady came out of the cabin and sat down on the back steps. She looked irritated. I stood there for a while longer watching them. I couldn't help but wonder what was going on.

After a bit, I turned around and made my way back to my truck and started to drive back down the mountain. Even though there were people at that cabin, I could tell it needed repairs.

I looked down the road by the lake as I drove by and spotted a car and a pickup truck now parked by the cabins there. This was my chance. I turned my truck down the road and parked behind them.

I saw a blonde lady and a burly looking man talking in the yard. I could hear a them talking as I walked up.

"There are the two cabins here, and then one other just a bit farther down the road. I think I'd like to get started on these first and then see about the other two up the mountain later,"she said.

They heard me approaching and turned. I smiled, and held out my hand, "Hello, folks. My name is Steven and I have heard that there may be some cabins up here that might need some renovation."

"Well, yes, maybe. Do you do construction?" asked Maggie.

"Yes, I do. I'm just kind of moving around currently, so I don't have anything steady, but I can assure you, I do good work."

"How about you leave me your number? I'm just now starting to look into what it would take to get the cabins repaired. I can always get back to you."

"Here's my card. I'll be in town and I'd love to have the opportunity to show you what I can do."

"Thank you," Maggie said, shaking my hand. "I'll get back with you."

"Thank you," I responded. I turned and left, hoping I'd hear back from her. I walked away a little, then crouched down to tie my boot. Hopefully I had made a good impression. I watched as Maggie turned back towards the inspector.

"Well, how often does that happen? Don't even have them inspected yet and already I have someone who wants to fix them up. How about I leave you to it?"

"No problem, Maggie, I'll look these cabins over and I'll give you a full report as soon as I can."

I watched as the inspector grabbed his flashlight and clipboard out of his truck.

That didn't sound too bad. I got up and made my way back to my truck.

"Thanks, I'll wait to hear from you." Maggie called out to the inspector as she walked away. I watched as she gave my business card another glance. Guess now I'd have to wait to see if she'd call me. I started my truck up and headed back to town.

CHAPTER THIRTEEN

EMILY

I HEARD the knocking at the door that evening as Maggie called out, "Hey Emily, it's me."

"Come on in," I shouted. I could hear her coming in. "I'm in the kitchen." I was pulling some rolls out of the oven. "Perfect timing. I just served up some mashed potatoes and pot roast with carrots. I hope you're hungry."

We both sat down at the table and starting serving our plates.

"Starving, actually. I've been busy today. Oh, this smells awesome," Maggie said while helping herself to a hot dinner roll.

"So, are you getting to the point where you need to find some permanent full-time help at the shop?"

"No, it's not so much that. I just spent some time up on the mountain today with the inspector. I met him up there and showed him the cabins.

"Oh, that's right. So how did it go?"

"Well, it's a start. He's going to take a look at the ones by the lake and get back with me. You and Mrs. Smithers were right, those, if they aren't too bad off, would make the best income potential."

"That lake is gorgeous up there. I'm surprised it hasn't been developed yet. I mean if I didn't live in the area, I'd love to vacation up there. Hiking, the view, the quiet."

"I know and hopefully I can make it even better. The cabins might offer some families the opportunity to make good summer memories. Of course, I know there isn't much of anything to do up there. So not sure how much of a draw it would be for a family, but a couple might enjoy the peace and quiet."

"No, don't forget the lake. I think families could really have some fun up there. Canoeing would be awesome; fishing, swimming. Last but not least, you can't forget campfires and s'mores."

"Well, we'll see what the inspector has to say." Maggie got a wistful look in her eyes. "I really hope this works out, I sure don't want to have to build them from the ground up. Oh, and by the way, guess who I talked to while I was up there?"

"Mrs. Smithers?"

"Ha! No, but she sure did like it up there, didn't she? She's such a sweetie. No, I talked to some guy named Steven, the construction guy."

"The same guy who was on my ghost tour and asking about construction work?"

"Yep, assuming that was him. Here, he gave me his card." She got up and rifled through her purse for the business card. "Here it is. Steven's Construction."

"Yep, that's the same one from my tour. I'm sorry to say, I'm not sure where I had put his card, but I do recognize it.

So, what did you think? Maybe bigger question, how did he find you?"

She paused and tipped her head to one side. "I don't know. I was at the lower cabins and he must have seen me there and decided to stop by. Anyway, I'll get the inspection report and then see how bad the damage is before I even think about hiring anyone. By the way, this is really good. I love these garlic mashed potatoes."

"Thanks, glad you like 'em." We continued our meal. After a bit she pushed her chair back from the table and took her plate into the kitchen. "I don't think I can eat another bite."

"That's a shame, because I have a yummy dessert," I said laughing. "Actually, it's not that bad, I thought we'd have something light after that meal. How do you feel about lemon ice cream? It has little lemon sandwich cookies crumbled up in it," I laughed, "but don't let me twist your arm or anything." I got up and took my plate to the kitchen.

"You know me, bring it on." I heard her laugh in the other room, "I'm just glad I don't eat like this every day."

I served us up both some bowls of lemon cookie crunch ice cream and brought it back to the dining room table.

"So, what do you think about the construction guy?" I just wanted to see if she picked up any bad vibes from him like I did.

"Well, I only talked to him for a couple of minutes. I really didn't give him much thought. I had my mind more on what work would be needed. You know me, one step at a time. I should hear back from the inspector soon."

"So, change of subject. What do you think, any chance you want to start running with me?"

"Ah no! You're so funny," Maggie said taking another bite of ice cream

"Oh, come on, you know you want to start exercising."

"Exercising maybe, but not running. How about I start with something smaller? Maybe something like weight lifting." She looked at me with a grin on her face. I can lift my coffee cup to drink it. It's about twelve ounces. How's that?" She laughed, spooning up some more ice cream.

"Why do I try?" I asked, shaking my head.

CHAPTER FOURTEEN

RENEE

MICHAEL SAT EATING some cold beans out of the can. "So how about we make some sandwiches and go for a hike?"

"I suppose, seeing as how there isn't anything to do up here. My gosh I think I'm going to die of boredom."

"Well you get your shoes on and grab your jacket. I'll make some sandwiches."

We left the cabin and wove our way down a narrow rough trail. It looked like it hadn't been used in a while and was almost nonexistent in some spots. "Michael, are you trying to kill me?"

"I thought you'd enjoy a hike. What's wrong?"

"What's wrong is, I expected a hike on a trial, not bush-whacking. And what's up with all these bugs? I think I'm being eaten alive," I said as I swatted a fly the size of a small rodent away from my face.

"Oh, come on Renee, where's your sense of adventure?"

"I know you didn't just say that." I glared at him.

Michael sighed. "Let's not fight. We've done enough of that lately and I'm tired of it."

"Maybe you should have thought of that before dragging me up to this godforsaken mountain. I would have been safe at home."

"I just didn't want to take any chances. You're important to me."

"If I'm so important to you, then why the heck did you report what the company was doing. You had to know it would lead to repercussions. Did you think they'd look at you and say, we're sorry Michael, we won't dump our toxic waste illegally anymore? And, oh by the way, congratulations for hacking into private documents." I was getting angrier now, and he had grown silent. We hiked and climbed in silence for several more minutes. All of a sudden, we came out onto a rocky outcrop. We both stopped dead in our tracks.

"Would you look at that?" Michael was gazing out onto a sapphire blue lake. "It doesn't look like it's changed at all."

"Did you know this was here?" The view had me stunned. It was amazing. I was looking down at a large, brilliantly blue lake far below us.

"Of course, I did, remember I used to come here with my parents."

We sat down on the rock and ate our lunch. There was not a soul in sight. The surface of the lake was silky smooth, and the whole area was surrounded by trees with mountains in the distance. A breeze stirred through the leaves of the trees and I could hear the pecking of a nearby woodpecker in one of the trees behind us. I felt totally peaceful and the tension I had been feeling started to drain away, until I remembered why I was here. This would be almost perfect if we weren't being hunted by a hired gunman. I certainly had a way of making myself come crashing back down to earth.

"Listen," Michael reached over to take my hand, "I know you haven't been happy with me lately. I also know you called a lawyer about a divorce before we left. And I want you to know I can't blame you if you want to leave, but at the same time, I'm going to try to win you back. I'm really sorry for getting you involved in any of this."

"I think it's just all the stress I've been under with everything going on, plus the new job. It's easy to pull apart during hard times. I'm sorry, I know I've let thing get to me."

He reached over and gave me a quick hug. "We're in this together and my priority has always been to keep you safe. I'm always here for you."

CHAPTER FIFTEEN

MAGGIE

A FEW DAYS LATER, I called Steven and asked if he could meet me up on the mountain to discuss renovations. He had already stopped by my shop and dropped off his references. People seemed pleased with his work.

"Hello, thanks for meeting me up here." I reached out to shake his hand.

"No problem, I'm glad you called." He reached up to adjust his cap.

"So, I inherited these cabins not too long ago and the inspector has given me some pretty good news about these three cabins. I thought maybe we could go over his report, let you look around, see if you could make some of these repairs, and give me an estimate on the costs. For now, I just going to start with this one cabin here, then if all goes well, I'll work on the others."

"How many do you have?"

"Cabins? Well I have five all together. Three here and then two further up the mountain. "

"Sounds like a good bit of work."

"Yes well, I don't want to get ahead of myself. I'm only going to start with this one for now. Want to take a look?"

"I'm ready when you are."

He followed me around to the back of the cabin. "It's going to have quite the view back there when you get some of that brush cleared out."

"I sure do hope so," I agreed. I turned to the steps, "Obviously I need some new steps here and the inspector recommended a new deck as well."

"Be careful of that next step," Steven pointed out a rotten spot on the next step.

We picked our way carefully up to the deck and took another moment to look out at the lake. "It's even prettier from up here, isn't it? Imagine being out here, kicking back with a couple of cold ones."

I turned to the door, and pulled out the key. It was a little stiff in the lock, but eventually turned. I automatically reached out for the light switch, but of course the cabin remained dark. The air inside was quite musty smelling.

"Boy, I guess this place has been closed up for a while now." Steven said looking around at the spider webs dangling in the corners.

We both turned to the windows, pushing back the moth-eaten curtains. No matter how slowly I tried pushing them apart, the dust went flying. I coughed reflexively, waving the dust away from my face.

"Sorry about the dust, maybe I should have come up here earlier and aired it out."

"No worries. I'm not afraid of a little dirt," he laughed.

"Looks like you've got a nice fire place here. I can check it out and make sure it's clean."

"Is that something you can do." I asked, continuing to look around the room.

"Sure can."

The couch and chairs in the room were upholstered in a now faded rose pattern. I thought to myself maybe they weren't faded, maybe it was just the amount of dust and grime that covered their surfaces. Either way, they would have to go. But the small hardwood table that sat in front of the windows, although it was equally dirty, appeared to still be in good shape.

"This is one of the problems over here." I said looking up at the ceiling. "There is a small leak in the roof and it's damaged this wall."

Michael came over, running his hand up the faded surface. "I can take care of that. Was that the only bad spot in the roof?"

"Yes, the inspector said surprisingly the rest of it was in fairly decent shape."

"These floors look good and solid." He said giving them a stomp. "They could use some sanding and refinishing though."

"Yes, you're right." Although with all the dirt and dust, it was hard to see exactly what shape they were in. I knew that was something I could take care of by myself.

We walked down the small hallway and into each of the two identical bedrooms and the bathroom that was nestled in-between them. The bathroom fixtures were old but in remarkably decent shape.

"Looks like the bedrooms are just in need of some cosmetic updating. The inspector said the plumbing actually appears to be in good shape too, so the bathroom looks like it could use a really deep cleaning. I not trying to totally update the cabins, at least not at this time." I said turning to look at him.

"I can understand that. I'll get the cabin livable and more important rentable so you can get some income coming in." He continued to look around the cabin's interior.

I'm sure he didn't mean to, but I thought his comment about making me some income was a little too personal. It didn't seem to bother me when Emily or Mrs. Smithers made similar comments. Maybe it was because he was a stranger. Or maybe I was just being overly sensitive. Steven had good references, so I needed to give him a shot, after all I did want to rent the cabins. I did want to make some income, otherwise what was the point?

"I can get started right away, especially if you can get the power on for my tools."

I nodded, "Yes, of course, I'll call the power company today."

"Okay, let me get my stuff out of the truck and I'll take some measurements and I can put together an estimate for you."

I felt a sense of excitement. I was actually going to have a cabin. Even better, a cabin by the lake. "Sounds good. If you will, stop by the shop in town and let me know what the damage is. We can firm up some plans then."

"I'll do it." He gave me a smile and reached out to shake my hand.

"I'll leave you to it then."

We walked back outside together and I stood on the deck for just a few more moments, soaking in the sunshine and admiring the lake, or at least what I could see of it.

"You know, I think I'd love to live up here. It's so quiet,

no one around, no nosey neighbors," he said, standing by me on the deck.

I watched as he walked back to his truck and came back with his tape measure and clip board.

I carefully picked my way back down the steps. "I'll get out of your way."

"I'll get the info to you as soon as I can."

"Thanks, I appreciate that." I looked at my watched, only to find it was a little later than I thought. I needed to get the shop open.

CHAPTER SIXTEEN

EMILY

I SHOWED up bright and early the next morning at Maggie's shop. The little bell rang as I entered, but Maggie was nowhere in sight.

"Good morning" I called out. "Anyone here?"

"Hey, good to see you." Maggie came around the corner from the back room.

"I come bearing gifts." I held out a cup to her and smiled.

"You are truly a friend." Maggie laughed, "would this be a caramel latte?"

"With extra caramel."

"This is so good." Maggie said taking a careful sip, "and extra hot, just like I like it."

"So, have you heard back from your construction guy?" I asked perching myself on one of her work stools.

"Not yet, but we were only up at the cabin yesterday morning. Figure he needs a little time to put the estimate together." Maggie took another sip of her coffee and set it out of the way. I could see she had supplies out on her work bench for an arrangement. "I'll be right back, I've got to get some roses from the front."

I heard the bell over her front door jingle.

"Hey, good morning Steven." Maggie greeted him, "So, what do you think?"

"It's definitely doable. I have your estimate here. I can leave it for you to look over and if you want to get some other estimates, that's fine too, just let me know what you decide."

I sat in the back, sipping my latte. It wasn't hard to hear their conversation. Maggie's shop was fairly compact.

"If I have you do the work, how long do you think it will take for the one cabin?"

"I'd say a couple of weeks at the most."

"Thanks for bringing this by. I've got your phone number, I'll look it over and I'll give you a call back."

"Not a problem. Thanks Maggie, I appreciate the opportunity to get some work up in this area. It's a really cute town, I might be interested in settling down here."

About that time, I heard Maggie's phone rang.

"I'll let you get back to business."

I heard the little bell jingle again. I peeked around the corner and watched as he walked out. I took my seat in the back room again. A few minutes later Maggie finished her call and came back in carrying some lovely white roses.

"Well that was him," Maggie said setting the roses down and reaching for her coffee. She looked over the estimate quickly and laid it to one side. "I'll look it over some more tonight, if it seems in order, I think, I'll hire him. He's going to replace the steps and decking. There is one small area of the roof that's leaking. I'll have him repair it and work on one of the walls in the cabin that has a little damage. I was also going to maybe have him work on the floors, sanding and refinishing. I know I could do them, but it's been so busy in the shop and I'd like to go ahead and get this one cabin finished up so I can start advertising. Even after Steven finishes the construction, we're still going to need to do a lot of cleaning, some painting and obviously work on new interior furnishings. I'd like to see if I can get some late spring or summer renters."

"We? Did I hear you say we?"

Maggie laughed, "Well I know how much you love painting walls and decorating. I sure didn't want to exclude you from the fun."

"Oh, you didn't want to exclude me?" I grinned at her.

"Are you going to repeat everything I say?"

"No, just the funny stuff." I laughed, "but seriously, of course, I'll be happy to help you out. Just tell me when and I'll be there for you."

"Thank you, and thanks for the coffee."

CHAPTER SEVENTEEN

ADAM

I DROVE BACK INTO TOWN. So far, this search was a bust. Where could this guy be? I had spent time in four small towns in the area, and now was right back where I started. My source was credible, or I thought he was. He always had good information for me in the past. In my line of work, there was no quitting and now was no exception. I was just going to have to continue looking.

My boss was becoming more and more impatient, even more than I was. I cruised slowly through town. I sure didn't want to draw any unwanted attention to myself. Rounding the town square, I finally pulled in, parked then sat there for a few minutes looking around and thinking. Another day or two here, then I'd have to consider this town a wash. I had checked out all the local hotels again, but no one checked in matching my target's description.

Glancing out my window, I looked up at the mountain. I thought for a minute, and wondered if Michael could be hiding out up there. I had driven up the mountain previously at least part of the way. The weather had been bad that night and I was forced to turn around. There wasn't much of anything up there, except a lot of trees. Now might be the time to venture back up there, but first, some food.

There was a little cafe that was just across the town square, who knows maybe I'd get lucky, and find my prey having lunch there. After all people have to eat. I exited my car and made my way casually toward the cafe. The shop windows beckoned with their brightly colored displays.

I crossed the street pretending to browse in each one, but I was really looking for my target. My orders were to get rid of the problem and I intended to carry them out. I had someone to find and I didn't give up, not when there was a target to find.

The little bell jingled as I entered the Little Copper Cafe and I was waved to a seat. The waitress hustled up to my table with a menu in hand and a smile on her face. Her name tag said her name was Claudette.

"I'll leave you this menu and let you look it over. Can I get you some coffee?"

"Yes, coffee."

She went off to get my coffee and I took a moment to glance around the cafe. For a little town, this cafe, seemed to do a pretty good business.

"Here you go." She placed the coffee and creamer on the table. "What can I get for you today?'

"How about a turkey bacon club with a side of fries."

"Coming right up."

The table at the window allowed me the opportunity to study each person as they walked by the window. Always looking. It was part of my training. From my seat, I could see most of the customers. I sipped my coffee, reviewing the room. Obvious tourists enjoying their lunches, a few business people, possibly from the courthouse, a couple of older men, probably locals, enjoying pie and coffee. A little while later Claudette came back with my lunch.

"This looks good, thanks." We both looked up as the door opened and the little brass bell over the door jangled.

"Hey Steven, welcome back. I see you decided to try out our lunch. Have a seat here." Claudette indicated a table by mine. The man named Steven sat with his back to me.

"What's your special today?" I heard him ask.

"We have meatloaf and mashed potatoes."

"Sounds perfect, I'll take it, with a coffee too, please."

Adam had only seen photos of his target, and this wasn't him. He was too muscular, and the wrong height. He also had the wrong hair color, although hair color was easily changed.

Later during the meal, Claudette stopped by the Steven's table again and they struck up a conversation.

"So, have you decided to stick around for a bit?"

"At least for a while. Remember you mentioned the cabins on the mountain that needed repair? Well, I put together a bid for the owner. We were up there yesterday looking over one of the cabins. Hopefully she'll like my bid and I can get started on the work."

His comments caught my attention.

"Well that is good news. I believe the owner has several cabins up there. That could keep you busy for a while."

"I can hope, and maybe I can make it back here for even more of your meals."

I listened to every word. That settled it. When I left here I'd make another trip up the mountain. It hadn't rained in a while, so the roads should be more passable. Claudette stopped by my table next to check on me.

"So how was it? It looks like you liked it." She glanced down at my empty plate.

"It was great, thank you. It looks like your place is pretty popular. I'll bet you see just about everyone passing through town." I typically wasn't much for chitchat, but I wanted to see how much she would talk.

She chuckled, "Well we do have other places to eat here, but I get a fair amount of traffic from both the tourists and locals. Guess I'm fortunate in that regard."

"Having good food helps, I'm sure. Listen, I'm supposed to be meeting a business associate up here. He said he was going to be coming to town. So far, I haven't seen him and I'm not able to get him on his cell either. I wonder if you've seen him?" I described the man I was looking for.

"I do get quite a lot of tourists in here, especially this time of year. We are getting ready to gear up for one of our yearly festivals. I'm not sure I've seen him though."

I noticed what I thought was just the briefest hint of wariness in her expression. She was sharp, that was for sure. That was it, I decided not to push. From my experience I knew she wasn't going to tell me anything. It would be worse if I made her suspicious. Time to go. I paid my check and left, again looking in all the shop windows along the way. Time for that ride up the mountain.

CHAPTER EIGHTEEN

ADAM

THE TEMPERATURE WAS COOL OUT, but a little warmer than it had been earlier in the week which caused me to roll up my sleeves as I worked my way back to where I was parked. My SUV was nondescript and I backed it out and pointed it in the direction of the mountain. The winding roads twisted back and forth. I took them carefully although I didn't expect to meet any on-coming traffic. There was the road that led to a lake. On my last drive up here, I had been by those three cabins before I was forced to turn around. It looked like all three where empty, except for the repairs being made on one of them. If I struck out further up the mountain, I'd swing back by here and give them another look. For now, I passed the lake road up, and chose to drive further up the mountain.

The higher I went the tighter the curves became. I drove silently down the road and ended up passing two cabins. Through the trees, I thought I spotted a faint wisp of smoke coming from the chimney of one. It needed to be checked out. The underbrush scraped the side of my vehicle as I turned it around and drove back down locating an overgrown side road. The ruts along this dirt road cause me to drive slowly, and finally forced me to stop altogether. I got out and entered the woods, taking my time. The leaves underfoot were soft and I moved quietly through the trees and brush. My training had prepared me for these situations, when silence was imperative.

Finally, I came to where I wanted to be. The underbrush was still thick and I was confident no one could see me. My suspicions were correct, one of these cabins were occupied. The woods around me fell silent as I crouched, and watched. There was a lady sitting on the back steps of the cabin. Her brown hair, glistening in the sun. She was long, lean and gorgeous. Her creased brow made her look anxious and worried. A man exited the cabin and sat on the steps by the lady. If I hadn't been trained my heartbeat might have quickened, like an animal spotting its prey. For now, I was content to watch from afar. The couple had no idea I was even there.

As the sun began to fade, the couple began to get a meal ready on an outside grill. I barely noticed how good it smelled. It was getting colder now that the sun was going down and I knew I needed to leave. Though I was skilled at being silent in the woods, I knew it would have harder making my way back to where I left my vehicle in the fading light. At last I knew where he was. I stood up to go, feeling the blood flow return to my lower limbs. That was when I got sloppy. I had only taken a few steps when a small branch snapped with a loud crack under my boot. I froze right where I was, and attempted to hear their conversation.

"Did you hear that?" Renee asked her husband

"It's the woods Renee, there are all sorts of noises out here at night. Calm down, don't be so paranoid."

"Paranoid? You're calling me paranoid? You drag me up here into this empty god forsaken back woods, because you think someone is after you. You have no idea of when we can even go back. And that makes me paranoid?"

"We haven't seen anyone close to here. We're fine," he sighed. "I'll try to get in touch with my contact and I'll get us back home as soon as I can. Please just be patient."

I watched their interaction. A minute later the lady got up and stalked into the cabin. Although I couldn't hear all of what they said, I got the jest of it. It was obvious that woman wasn't happy. I hadn't expected to find him up there with a woman. This would complicate the situation. There could be no witnesses. I'd have to report this. Would I now have two targets?

CHAPTER NINETEEN

RENEE

THERE WAS a slight breeze blowing the tops of the tall pines. The birds could be heard chirping as I came out onto the back porch. It was about mid-morning. It was easy to sleep late up here, with the quiet and nothing much to do.

"What are you doing? I thought you wanted some fresh air," Michael asked when I came right back into the cabin.

"Well, I changed my mind." I plunked back down on the cot and picked up the book that I had been reading.

"Would you like to go for a hike? It's nice and cool out this morning. I think I saw some deer tracks out back this morning. Maybe we can spot some wildlife."

"No, I think I'm good with staying put right now." I sighed, "This place is really lovely" I said putting my book aside. "I think I'd really enjoy it more if our circumstances were different."

"I know we loved it up here when I was a kid. Dad would take me fishing in the lake. Mom loved relaxing in the peace and quiet. Listen, if you don't want to go for a walk, how about I fix us some food."

"I'm actually not too hungry right now."

"Well that might be a good thing, we are going to need to go easy on our eating."

I sat up on the side of my cot, and could feel a bit of anxiety rising. There was only so many days we could eat peanut butter sandwiches or canned spaghetti. As it was now, we only cooked about once a day. I really missed having a normal kitchen and good food. "So, speaking of our dwindling supplies, I was thinking I could take a trip into town today, pick up us some groceries. Maybe I could make a call to the prosecutor and check the status of the case."

"You know we shouldn't show our faces too much. I was hoping we could ration what supplies we have here for another couple of days. After that I know we'll have to go to town."

"But I could go, just by myself. After all, you're the one they are looking for, not me."

Michael shook his head at me. "No, it's too dangerous. I don't want to put you in danger, Renee."

"Look Michael I know you didn't mean to, and you're doing the right thing, but you've sort of already put me in danger, just being here. And who knows, they may not know anything about me. They very well could just be looking for you. I'll be quick. Just a quick trip to town and right back. No one will hardly notice me at all. I promise I'll be careful."

He sighed heavily and dropped his head, "Renee, I'm sorry, you know I never meant to involve you in any of this. If you promise to be careful, really careful I mean, you can make a quick run into town."

I walked up to him, taking his hands and looking him in

the eyes, "look, we are going to be okay. I know I've given you a hard time about all this, but you really are doing the right thing. While I'm in town, I'll make the call and see how the case is going. Who knows, they may be able to give us the all clear." After a quick kiss on his cheek I grabbed my purse and keys. I was anxious to get going before he changed his mind.

I watched as Michael walked to the edge of the road. It seemed like an eternity before he motioned an all clear and I eased the car out from behind the cabin. "I promise I'll be careful" I told him, reaching out my hand to touch his before driving off. He stood in the road watching me drive away. The road twisted and turned down the mountain and I was so excited to be away from the cabin. My mind swirled with thoughts of a good dinner, not to mention the pending call to the prosecutor. The possibility of going home soon, made me practically giddy. Michael and I were working on our relationship and hopefully things between us would continue to improve, especially after this mess with Prism was over.

Turning into town I spotted a pay phone. We had left our cell phones at home. Michael didn't want anyone to be able to locate us. It's a wonder this town even had a pay phone. Guess it was my lucky day. Pulling the car over, I hopped out, made my call and received great news. The prosecutor told me, the police had raided the company. He said they were reviewing the evidence now including emails and photos. Charges were hopefully going to be filed soon against the chemical company and then we should be safe to return home. I was ecstatic. Michael and I could get our lives back. With any luck, I'd get back to my clients soon. I had just recently started work at the new salon and was anxious to become established again. The feelings of anger and resentment were still fresh when I thought of why I had to change salons at all, but at the time, it seemed to be the only solution. I sighed, trying to put all the bad thoughts aside. Pretty soon this whole ordeal would be over.

I made a stop at the local grocery store, just to pick up a few things. We definitely needed some new batteries for the flash lights as they were getting dim. It was going to be so nice to get back home and get back to electricity. I decided to splurge for dinner, after all we had something to celebrate. Leaving the grocery store, I spotted a barbeque restaurant and thought Michael would love nothing better than to eat some good smoked barbeque ribs. I ordered our dinner even including apple cobbler for dessert. For once, things were looking up for us and I couldn't keep the smile off my face, after all we were going to celebrate tonight. I turned the car back up toward the mountain and hoped that Michael wouldn't be too worried. My quick trip, seemed to have taken me a little longer than I had anticipated.

CHAPTER TWENTY

MICHAEL

HOW LONG WAS it going to take her? I glanced at my watch and continued to pace back and forth in the cabin. I knew I was going to be a nervous wreck until Renee got back. Maybe it would make the time pass faster, if I did something useful, so I started chopping a little wood. After all we always needed wood for the fireplace. My axe thunked into the stump and I bent over to pick up the wood now scattered around on the ground. I brought a load of it inside and dumped it in the box by the fireplace. Maybe if everything worked out Renee and I could come back up here and really enjoy the area. Who was I kidding, she'd never want to come back up here, too many bad memories were now tied to this place. Hopefully we could find a new vacation spot.

I turned to go back out, but came to a sudden stop when I saw a figure standing in the doorway. My heart started to pound, because it was obvious that it wasn't Renee. The figure was obviously a man.

"Can I help you?" I sputtered

The man didn't say anything. The sun was shining brightly behind him and I couldn't make out his features.

"You should have just left."

"Who are you? What do you mean? I did leave." I remembered the ax outside. Even if I had it with me, I wasn't much of a fighter.

"Listen if this is about Prism, we can talk about it. I really don't know anything." I was going to have to try to bluff my way out of this. Maybe I could talk to the guy and convince him that I really wasn't a threat to the company.

The man in the doorway took a step forward and raised his right arm. I backed up instinctively, putting my hands up, but it was too late. Everything went black.

CHAPTER TWENTY-ONE

ADAM

MY CAR WAS PARKED LESS than a block away when I spotted the car. It was turning into town from the mountain road. There was a female driving and it looked like she was alone in the car, which meant one thing. My target was alone, up on the mountain. Time to go to work. I started my car and headed up the now familiar mountain road, remembering exactly where I needed to go. This time I would find him alone. I was ready to eliminate the threat and head home. My boss had grown impatient and now wanted the situation taken care of quickly and quietly. And besides, all these little towns had getting old.

Even though it probably wasn't necessary, I picked my way through the woods like I had done on my prior trip. The sounds of chopping wood rang out and I knew I was getting close. Another few minutes and I the cabin came into view. I paused a brief moment before I stepped out of the tree line, checking to make sure I was safe.

I left the cabin, picked my way back through the woods to my vehicle and made my way down the mountain. My work here was done and I'd never have to come back here again. It was still fairly early and if I was lucky I could be half way back to civilization before I needed to stop for the night. Trooping through the woods had made me thirsty, so I pulled into a local gas station. I could stop for gas, pick up something to drink and be on the road before anyone found the body. With my vehicle gassed up, I climbed back in eager to be on my way. I couldn't believe it. It wouldn't start. I tried again, but with no luck. What in the world was going on?

The mechanic came walking out, wiping his hands on a rag, "Need some help?" He asked me.

"It was fine when I pulled in here. Now it's not starting."

"I'll take a look."

Pretty soon, he looked at me, and confirmed there was a problem with the computer. This couldn't be happening.

"Which direction to your car rental agency?"

"Ah, sorry. This is Copper Ridge you're talking about here mister. We don't have a car rental agency here."

"Great, just great. Well how long will it take to make the repairs? Can you even make the repairs?"

He took off his cap, scratched his head before putting his cap back on. "I can, but I'd have to get the part from a dealer. Maybe a couple of days. Again, this is what happens when you live in a small town."

This was going from bad to worse. "Sure ok, get it fixed as fast as you can." I turned around, rubbing the back of my neck, it was a habit I had. Guess I was going to need another night at the hotel after all.

"Do you have a place to stay? Need a ride somewhere?" the mechanic asked.

"Yes, maybe out to the hotel on the bypass."

"One of my guys'll run you out there."

"Sure, and I'll pay extra if you put a rush on the repairs. I've got some business I need to take care of."

The mechanic called one of his guys who drove the me out to the hotel. I booked my room and thought, I'd never live in a small town. Nothing about this job had been normal. Even though the closest town was about thirty miles away, it wasn't much bigger than this place. Come to find out, it didn't have a car rental agency either. What did these people do when they needed a rental car? For now, I'd get some dinner and lie low. I was a professional and good at being invisible. Of course, I usually had everything I needed too, which included a vehicle.

CHAPTER TWENTY-TWO

RENEE

DRIVING the route up and down the mountain was becoming more familiar, I thought as I pulled the car around to the back of the cabin. Michael was going to be so excited when he heard the news. Glancing quickly at the cabin, I noticed the back door standing open, but that wasn't unusual. We left it open frequently to let in some additional light. With the power off and the front drapes closed, it could get really dark in the cabin.

"Michael," I called out excitedly, wanting to tell him my good news but got no response. Grabbing the barbeque, I hopped out of the car. But what I saw next, stopped me dead in my tracks. I heard what sounded like screams, and realized the sound was coming from me. My excitement evaporated; the celebratory dinner now long forgotten. I rushed in, but knew instantly it was too late. There was nothing I could do. I had to get the police.

I drove like a mad woman down the mountain, crying

all the way, my tears making it difficult to see. The car swerved from side to side after taking one of the curves too quickly and I struggled to keep it on the narrow mountain road. Michael had been right, but even so, it was hard to process. This couldn't be happening. Obviously, he had told me his life was in jeopardy, but I never believed that something would actually happen. I was stunned.

Tears continued to stream down my face as I rode silently in the police car back up the mountain. Previously the surrounding forest seemed quiet and serene, now it seemed dark and sinister. This wasn't real.

Time passed, but I didn't know how much, nor did I really care. The police and investigators were in the cabin. The coroner had been called and I sat alone in the back of one of the patrol cars. The police had wanted me to stay at the station while they went up to the cabin, but I wanted to come back. I longed to be close to Michael, but he was gone now. Fresh tears rolled down my cheeks again. We had our fights like any couple, but I couldn't imagine life without him.

The yellow crime scene tape was swaying in the breeze, mocking me with its color and movement. I watched the detective and police officers as they came out of the cabin and stopped just short of the car I was in.

"So, do we know who owns this cabin?" the detective asked.

The other officer flipped open his notebook, "We checked the records. Seems like the cabin is owned by Maggie Sanders. Looks like the title was transferred to her pretty recently too."

"Is that the Maggie who owns the flower shop?"

"Yes, that's her." The policeman confirmed.

"Can you call her and have her meet me at the police station in a bit?"

"Sure thing."

I watched the policeman walk off and the detective headed my way. He opened my door and I tried to focus on what he was saying.

"We are all finished here Mrs. Jameson. Again, I'm very sorry for your loss. I'm going to have one of my officers drive you back to the station. I need to get a statement from you, that is, if you're up to it."

"Yes, sure," I mumbled and nodded my head.

The policeman got back in the car and as we drove off, I took one final look at the cabin as another tear coursed down my cheek.

CHAPTER TWENTY-THREE

RENEE

I SAT in a stark looking interrogation room, trying to hold it together. Someone had wrapped a blanket around my shoulders, but I still couldn't seem to stop shaking. How could my life have come apart like this? The thoughts swirled in my mind. Sure, Michael and I had our share of marital trouble, but all couples had trouble from time to time. Ours might not be the typical troubles most couples have, but we were trying to work our way through them. What was I going to do? He couldn't be gone. How could the company had actually found us? We had been so careful. Maybe if I had been there we could have gotten away. Maybe Michael wouldn't be dead. Maybe we'd both be dead.

The door opened, the detective entered the room and took a seat across the table from me.

"I'm Detective Mason. Thank you for doing this now. I

know this must be very difficult for you, but any information you can provide would be very helpful."

"Yes of course," I nodded.

"Did your husband have any enemies?"

"As a matter of fact, he did. You see about a month ago, Michael was at work, he works," I paused, looking down at my hands "worked for Prism Chemical Company. He came across some emails that talked about toxic waste dumping. Illegal toxic waste dumping." I paused again, "Michael might have hacked into one of their secure systems and discovered that bit of information. He said he was trying to get a better position in the company. Seems like he wasn't the only one at the company who was taking short cuts. Anyway, he read some emails that he wasn't supposed to. He soon realized that he couldn't use the information like he thought he'd be able to. Then the threats started. I know it wasn't right, but I tried to persuade him to just let it go. Eventually, he reported his findings to the authorities, and then brought us here to hide out. I had come into town today to call the prosecutor and check the status of the case. He actually had given me good news. He told me they were reviewing the evidence now and he anticipated arrests would be made soon. We were going to be going back home soon. I just found out today. Michael didn't even know yet. Michael, was sure they had sent someone to find him. So far, we hadn't seen anyone or anything suspicious, but obviously we missed something. They must have had someone tracking us. Someone found him and took care him. Now I'm not even sure they can proceed with their case. Michael may have died for nothing."

Tears started to roll down my cheeks and Detective Mason moved a box of tissues across the table top, and sat patiently waiting for me to compose myself.

"Did you see anything or anyone up on the mountain today?

"No, not really. I mean there isn't much of anything up there."

"How about any other days?"

"Well on occasion we have been walking and have seen a red pick-up truck up there. But I think it belongs to whoever is working on one of the cabins by the lake. The truck was there today, I remember seeing it on my way into town."

"We'll track the owner down and see what he can tell us. And how about your relationship with your husband; how was it?"

I seemed a little taken aback by the question. "I love my husband. He's a good man. I mean, we had our good times and bad times like anyone else," I paused. "You can't possibly think I had anything to do with this."

About that time the door opened, "Detective, the owner of the cabin is here."

"Will you excuse me for a minute and I'll be right back," he got up exiting the room.

I nodded, wondering now if whoever owned the cabin would also press charges for trespassing. But it didn't matter, nothing mattered now. Michael was gone and I felt utterly lost. The wool was scratchy again my cheek as I pulled the blanket tighter around my shoulders. For now, I felt like that blanket was the only thing holding me together.

CHAPTER TWENTY-FOUR

EMILY

I GOT to town a little early and went to meet Maggie at her shop, "Are you ready?"

"Yep, coming." Maggie called from the back room. "Claudette and I are excited to have you on the committee this year. You know the Copper Ridge Fall Bazaar is an exciting time around here. We get a lot of tourists in for the event."

"So, what is this fall bazaar anyway?"

"It's a sort of kick off to the holiday shopping season here in town. It's a well-known event around this part of the state too. The shop owners put out a lot of new merchandise, they offer pretty good bargains, and we have music and food in the town square. We also have some people that set up booths in the square to sell home made goods. Overall, we just get a lot of folks coming into town to eat and shop. You're going to love it. Some folks just come in for the day, others stay overnight. It's a nice boost to the economy. You might even get some new folks in for your ghost tours."

Maggie locked up her shop and we walked down the street to The Little Copper Cafe, where we were meeting with Claudette and a couple of other folks on the committee. This was my first fall in Copper Ridge and so far, I absolutely loved it. It was only a short walk down the sidewalk to the cafe so there wasn't much time to take in all the fall colors. We knocked on the door and waited for Claudette. It was about an hour past her normal midafternoon closing time and would give us a quiet place to meet.

"Oh, my goodness, it smells good in here. What are you baking?" I asked as Claudette opened the door for us. The aroma of fresh baked goods and cinnamon filled the cafe.

She hurried back into the kitchen and came out with a plate of tarts. "Hope you ladies are ready for a snack, because I need some taste testers. This is my new recipe for cinnamon apple tartlets. I butter the top crust and sprinkle cinnamon sugar on it. My secret ingredient is a little vanilla in with the apples. Tell me what you think? Oh wait, I almost forgot, we need ice cream." She hurried back to the kitchen. Maggie and I looked at each other and laughed.

"She knows us so well. We'll do anything for food."

Claudette came back and scooped out ice cream and plopped it on top of each hot tartlet. We waited for her to come back and then dug in.

"Oh my goodness, Claudette, this is wonderful." I closed my eyes and savored the first bite. Flaky buttery crust with warm apple filling and a little bite of cinnamon coupled with the vanilla ice cream made for an absolutely delicious combination.

Maggie looked at me and laughed, "It takes so little to make you happy."

"Well I'm glad I can make you happy with my cooking. Now, ladies, why don't we get to business," Claudette said.

"Aren't we going to wait for the others?" I asked between bites.

"No unfortunately it's just going to be us today. The other ladies sent the apologies, but I told them I could bring them up to speed later."

"Did the banners come in?" Maggie asked looking over at Claudette.

"Yes. Two of them. We'll get them hung up across the road in and out of town. The extra lights will be hung up in the square. We have the stages ordered. Maggie what's the update on the music?"

Maggie pulled some paperwork out of her purse. Here are a list of bands and the time slots for their performance. I think it's going to be even better than last year.

I listened while the two ladies discussed the food, and the layout for the local vendors that were going to set up booths in the square and other details.

"This sounds like a really special event. I'm looking forward to it." I reached for a little extra cream for my coffee.

Maggie's cell phone rang and she excused herself to take the call. We heard her say, "yes, I'll be right there." She hung up and came back.

"Sorry ladies to cut this short, but I'm wanted down at the police station."

"Why? What happened?" as if it were any of my business.

"Well it seems like there has been some type of incident up at one of my new cabins. That's all they'd say. I'll see you guys later. Claudette thanks for the dessert. It's a winner." She turned to leave.

"Hey wait for us." Claudette was up and moving. "We're not letting you go by yourself."

"I hope your construction guy didn't have an accident or anything." I hurried to catch up with them, shoveling the last bite of dessert into my mouth. "Ha! Mustn't let it go to waste."

CHAPTER TWENTY-FIVE

CLAUDETTE

I TURNED to lock up and we all made our way down to the police station. It wasn't that far away, but then again nothing was far away in Copper Ridge, but I think we made the walk there in record time. As we hurried in, an officer at the front desk greeted us, saying he'd get Detective Mason. We didn't have to wait long before he came down the hallway.

"Maggie, sorry you had to come down here." He reached out to shake Maggie's hand.

"No problem, but what's this all about? I hope nothing bad has happened to Steven."

"Who's Steven?"

"Steven is the man I hired to work on one of my cabins up by the lake. He's doing some construction."

"No, it's not Steven. Can you come with me, we can talk a little more privately?"

"Yes, sure." She started to follow him and I automatically started to follow.

"Ah, is it ok if the ladies come with me?" Maggie asked pointing to us?

He turned around to look over at us, "yes, if you're sure you don't mind."

We all followed Detective Mason down the hallway to the empty conference room. "Have a seat ladies." He paused until we got settled in our seats, then looked over at Maggie. "I'll get right to the point. There has been a murder at one of your cabins."

"What!" Emily yelped, she couldn't seem to help herself.

We looked over at Maggie, her mouth was open and the color had drained out of Maggie's face. I reached over, took hold of Maggie's hand, and gave it a squeeze.

Detective Mason continued, "It seems like you had a couple hiding out in one of your cabins high up on the mountain."

"Hiding out?" Maggie stammered.

"Yes, it's an involved story, but apparently the man that was killed was being sought after by someone, possibly for seeing something illegal. We think someone might have been tying up loose ends so to speak. Of course, it's all still under investigation, but as the property owner we wanted you to be aware. The crime scene is still sealed off for now." He paused again, "I can let you know when you can have access to it again."

Poor Maggie, she looked stunned. "Sure, no problem. You do whatever you need to do."

Had I heard him correctly? I looked at the ladies and then over at Alex. "So Alex, I mean Detective, you said there was a couple up at the cabin. What happened to the man's wife?"

Alex paused and glanced over at me. "She's here. I'm getting a statement from her while it was all still fresh. She's claiming to have been here in town when the murder took place."

"Oh my." I gasped.

"Of course, she's going to need to stay in town at least for a few days while we continue our investigation. I'm going to have one of my men run her out to a hotel."

"Alex, why don't you let me take her home with me? I have a spare room and I remember what it was like when I lost my Henry. This has got to be an incredibly difficult time for her. I really feel for her."

"Absolutely not!" Alex looked at me like I had lost my mind. "That is not a good idea."

"And tell me why not?" Unless he had a really good answer, I wasn't going to let this go.

"She admitted to having fights with her husband. She is a suspect until proven otherwise."

"Oh, pish posh. Having fights with your spouse doesn't make someone guilty of murder. And thank goodness for that. Henry and I had some doozies in our day. Thank goodness they all ended happily for both of us. You know, what they say about making up..." The thought of my Henry brought a smile to my face.

Detective Mason held up his hand and interrupted me. "Claudette, no, you don't know this lady. I don't know her and I'm not sure what she is capable of."

"Well, how about this, can I get a glimpse of her through your one-way window thingy. I'm a really good judge of character. I'll watch and you go ask her and see what she says and I'll take it from there. I'd just hate the thought of her being cooped up in a hotel room all by herself." I crossed my arms and leveled my gaze at him, "Should we get the chief?" Oh, the perks of small-town living. The police chief and I go way back and he definitely knew better than to argue with me.

Detective Mason, sighed heavily. I watched as he grudgingly stood up and walked out of the room. He seemed to know it was a losing battle to argue with me anymore.

Emily had been sitting there watching our exchange. She leaned forward in her seat and whispered, "Alex? You call him Alex?"

I smiled down at her as I got up from my chair to follow Detective Mason down the hallway. I leaned over knowing I had won, "Well dear I've known him practically all his life. I try to remember to call him Detective here, but I sometimes forget."

I heard a little giggle from Emily as I walked out the door. Detective Mason was standing a little way down the hallway, waiting for me with his arms crossed.

"I can't talk you out of this can I?" Alex's brow was furrowed with worry.

"It'll be alright, just let me listen to her."

Procedure or not, Detective Mason, got me situated in the room next to where Renee was seated. The one-way window allowed me to watch her as she sat there, the look of shock, disbelief on her face. He re-entered the interrogation room. Renee still clutched her blanket tightly around her shoulders.

"Mrs. Jameson, sorry to keep you waiting."

Her eyes were red and swollen from crying, her face was blotchy. He was all professional with her.

"You're free to go for now, but we need you to stay in town for a few days in case we have more questions."

"Okay, I can do that," she nodded. "Do you know of a good place to stay? I think I remember some hotels out on the freeway. I don't have a cell phone, but I can call and let you know where I am."

"Yes, you're right. There are a couple of them out there. We can get you to one out there if you're not up to driving." He paused and looked over at the window I was behind. "Or, if you want to consider it, I have an old friend who is willing to put you up while you're here. She's a really sweet lady who owns our local cafe. You would actually be just down the street from here."

"Well I don't know, I mean I don't want to cause any trouble or put her out. No that's okay. I'll find me a hotel."

A moment later I was out of my room and down the hall. I was satisfied with what I'd had seen and heard. I recognized that look on her face. The look that said she had just lost her husband, someone she loved. It was the way I looked after I lost Henry. "It's no trouble at all." I said from the doorway. I took another step into the room. "Let me help you." I gave her an encouraging smile and reached out a hand.

"Thank you. But are you sure? I don't want to be any trouble."

"Detective is she finished here for now?"

"Yes, and thanks Claudette. Call me or call the station if you need anything." He admonished me on the way out.

With my arm around my new charge, we started down the hallway. "Let's get you back to my place and I can get you settled. I can make you a cup of tea or find you something stronger if you like." We got to the lobby and Emily and Maggie were waiting for us there. There were quick introductions made. "Ladies," I said looking at Emily and Maggie, "if you don't mind I'm going to get Renee back to the house. She's had a long day and I'm sure she'd appreciate some rest.

CHAPTER TWENTY-SIX

EMILY

THE NEXT DAY I stopped at the cafe right before Claudette was due to close up. I stood by the counter and waited until she was free.

"I just wanted to stop by and check on you and Renee. How's everything going?"

"I'm doing fine. There was no reason for you, Maggie or Alex to worry about me." She laughed, "Alex was down here early this morning and Maggie came in right before lunch. I knew I'd be ok. Renee on the other hand has had some rough moments. You know it's especially hard just being idle. Sometimes it helps to be busy. Hold that thought, let me check out this customer and I'll be right back."

Claudette took care of her last customer and locked the door.

"Why don't you have a seat and I'll be right back," she said hurrying off to the kitchen.

Claudette came back carrying a brownie covered in caramel sauce. "You want a cup of coffee to go with that?"

"I can get it, why don't you cut yourself a brownie too and come and sit down with me. I'll bring you a coffee too."

"Let me go see if Renee would like to come down and join us."

Claudette ran upstairs while I poured coffee and got creamer. In just a moment Claudette returned with Renee who looked a little pale.

"Here we go ladies." I came out of the kitchen with a tray of brownies, hot caramel sauce, cups of coffee and brought them back to our table. "Hey Renee, my name is Emily, we met yesterday."

"Yes, of course. I was a little out of it."

Claudette passed around silverware and napkins, "ladies, dig in and I hope you enjoy. Chocolate can't take away all your troubles, but it sure can help."

We ate in silence for a few minutes. "So how did your day go Claudette?" I asked, pouring a little more caramel on my brownie.

"Phew, I sure was busy today. My part time waitress is going to be unavailable this week and I'm running like crazy."

I looked at Claudette and nodded my head toward Renee. She looked puzzle for a moment then the light dawned in her eyes. "Say, Renee, I'm not sure you'll want to or feel like it, but what do you think about helping me out here in the cafe?" She paused for a moment and then hurried on. "Please don't feel obligated. You are welcome to stay here with me, regardless of what you decide, but it might help to keep your mind occupied."

"Oh." Renee seemed to be in her own little sad world.

She lifted her head, her face seemed to brightened a bit. "Did you say, help you here?"

"But only if you want. I'd pay of course. I'd never expect you to work for free or anything like that. But if you don't feel up to it, I certainly understand."

"Actually, yes, I think I'd like that. It would be good for me to be busy right now. It's hard just sitting around, it gives me too much time to think." She paused looking up from her coffee cup and gave us a slight smile. "And on the up side, you'll be happy to know I won't be a complete klutz, I used to be a waitress. It helped me work my way through school for a bit."

I smiled at both of them, "Well then, it's settled. Congratulations Claudette, it looks like you have a new employee, even if it's just for a short time."

"Do you think the detective will let me go back up to the cabin? Most of my clothes and things are up there. I don't really want to go back up there, but I need some of my things, especially if I'm going to be helping out here."

"Do you want me to go up there for you. I can get your things and bring them back, if you'd like." I volunteered. Maggie and I can ask Detective Mason if he will let us go back up there. We'd be happy to get everything packed up."

"I don't want to be a bother. I'm sure you have things to do, without being bothered with me."

"It's not a bother, really." I looked at her directly. "You know since I've moved here, I've learned something about friendships and reaching out a hand to someone who might need it. Collecting your things is not a big deal for me, but if it helps you, then it's the least I can do."

I watched as Renee wiped away a tear. "Thanks, to you both. Claudette if you hadn't offered your home, I'd be cooped up in some hotel room, staring at four walls and going crazy. And Emily, thank you. If you wouldn't mind, I'd really appreciate if you could make a trip back up to the cabin for me. I don't want to go back there at all. I really appreciate your kindness."

"Then it's settled." I gave Claudette a smile, looks like we have a plan.

We finished up our brownies and I promised I'd let Renee know what I heard from Detective Mason.

CHAPTER TWENTY-SEVEN

CLAUDETTE

THE NEXT DAY Renee started helping me out in the cafe, wearing a crisp new uniform. I watched her periodically and thought she was a real natural. Things were going so much smoother for me today with the extra help. Around lunch time the little bell tinkled and I saw Steven's familiar face as he came in the cafe. I grabbed a menu and went to greet him.

"Welcome back, glad to see you. Need some time to look at the menu?" I asked showing him to a table.

"No, how are your burgers?"

"The best around, if I do say so myself. We have a three cheese, a grilled onion and bacon burger or our barbecue burger."

"How about the grilled onion and bacon, and a side of fries too."

"Coffee?"

"Definitely."

"Coming right up."

I moved behind the counter to turn in Steven's order. Renee was coming by with the coffee pot. "Table two by the window needs some coffee."

"No problem" Renee turned and stopped dead in her tracks.

As I looked over at her, I saw all the color had drained from Renee's face and she was frozen where she stood. "Renee, what's wrong?"

Renee turned around, her hands were shaking and she put the coffee pot back on its burner. "Claudette, I'm not feeling so good right now. I think I need to take a break. I'm sorry." Renee turned and hurried back through the kitchen door.

The door which led in and out of the kitchen, swung back and forth as Renee retreated. I sure hoped she felt better soon. She remembered how I was affected by waves of grief after the sudden passing of my husband. That must have been what had happened to Renee, but for whatever reason I had an uneasy feeling. Maybe it was just me being a mother hen and my worrying nature acting up. The little bell rang again and I didn't have a chance to think about it anymore. There were orders to take and plates to serve. I'd take being busy with customers over an empty cafe any day.

A little while later Renee returned. "Claudette I'm so sorry, I don't know what got into me."

"Don't you worry about it my dear. You work when you feel like it and when you need a break, you just let me know." It continued to be a busy afternoon, almost right up until closing. It would have been a rough day without Renee. I realized what a good worker she had turned out to be, although I still couldn't help but wonder if there was something else going on. Something besides grief, something Renee was holding back.

CHAPTER TWENTY-EIGHT

EMILY

MAGGIE and I stopped by the police station to see if we were cleared to return to Maggie's cabin. We didn't have to wait too long before Detective Mason came out to greet us.

"What can I do for you today, ladies?"

"We were wondering if it was okay if we go back to the cabin to gather up Renee's things. She's running out of clothes and didn't want to go back up there."

"How is she doing over there with Claudette?" He asked. "I haven't been down there today to check on them."

Maggie laughed, "Claudette put her to work."

"Sounds like something she'd do." He admitted.

"Yes, we're finished with the scene. Feel free to collect her stuff from up there. I've got to make a quick call, but I'll meet you up there and help you out."

"Sounds like a plan, we'll see you there." We left the police station and headed up to the cabin that Renee had been hiding out in.

"I had such high hopes for these cabins. It doesn't seem so pleasant up here now." Maggie was looking out the window with a somber look on her face.

"Don't worry, Maggie. I know it seems like this now, just give it some time. Get the cabins cleaned up and then see what you think." I was trying to encourage her.

"I sure hope so since I'm getting the first one fixed up now."

Maggie pulled the car up in front of the cabin and we sat there looking at it. The sun was shining, the birds were chirping and yet the yellow crime scene tape, reminded us of what couldn't be forgotten. By the time we got out of the car, we heard another vehicle approaching. Detective Mason drove in and parked behind us.

"Okay ladies, just beware, the interior has not been cleaned up."

This made my stomach lurch. Come on, I told myself, you volunteered for this, just get it over with. We entered the cabin together. Even in the meager light, it was impossible to miss the dark stain now soaked into the old wooden floor. We looked about the cabin. It contained very little, air mattresses, sleeping bags, cots, lanterns, clothing and a meager amount of groceries.

"Well Renee certainly didn't bring much with her." I looked around, thinking this wouldn't take long.

"No, she sure didn't. Here's a suitcase." Maggie spotted it in the corner. It didn't take us long to pack up her few articles of clothing.

"What should we do with Michael's belongings?" I asked looking at Detective Mason.

"It's okay we can pack it up, the police are finished with everything here."

Maggie and I packed up the clothing and Detective

Mason started gathering up the camping equipment. He was stowing it in the trunk of Maggie's car. She and I finished up in no time. Maggie looked around the cabin when we got ready to leave. It's sad that such a tragedy took place here. As she walked out of the cabin she looked at the door.

"So, Detective, did Renee ever mention how they happened to pick this cabin?" Maggie asked him.

"Yes, seems like Michael used to come up here with his parents when he was a kid. Renee told me they used to come up here to this cabin every summer to enjoy some hiking, and fishing."

"Well how did he get in? It doesn't look like the door lock was damaged."

Detective bent down and lifted a rock, there was the key to the cabin. "Renee said he told her this is where the key was always kept."

Maggie's mouth fell open. "I wonder if the other cabins have keys outside them too. Guess I should check. I mean, it won't keep anyone out if they really want to get in, but still."

"And you mentioned to me the other day that you had someone doing repairs on a cabin up here."

"That's right. I have three cabins down by the lake. I've got a guy working on one of them for me. His name is Steven." She responded to the detective.

"Renee had mentioned seeing a truck down that way. I looked down that way when I drove up here, but I didn't see a truck or anything. I'll come back up here. I really need to speak with him. Well, ladies I have a couple of more box to get inside and then we can go."

Maggie glanced at her watch, then spoke up. "Guys, I'm sorry I have to go. I forgot I have a customer that I'm supposed to meet and I'm late already. Can you guys can drive back together?"

"Of course," Detective Mason spoke up. He turned to go back in the cabin.

Maggie stepped down off the back porch, and I gave her a quizzical look. She shrugged her shoulders and had that mischievous look on her face. I couldn't believe her. She made a shooing motion with her hands and hurried off to get in her car.

Detective Mason's came out a couple of minutes later carrying the last two boxes. "I looked around and I think this is the last of it."

"I hope you don't mind driving me back, Maggie was in a bit of a hurry to get back." I couldn't help but wonder what in the world she was up to.

He loaded up the last load in the back seat of his car and then stepped back and held the front door open for me.

"Not at all, happy to have the company." He did have a nice smile I thought.

He climbed in the car and I wondered if he'd spill the beans on the status of the investigation. "So, any luck on the case so far?"

"We have a couple of leads, and of course we've spoken to the prosecutor who is working the case against the chemical company."

He stopped himself all of a sudden. "Why is it you can pick my brain so easily?"

"Just lucky I guess," giving him a grin. I lowered my head thinking about the conversation that I had previously overheard in the grocery store between Renee and Michael.

Detective Mason looked over, "Hey what's up? What aren't you telling me?"

I hesitated for a moment. "Well to be honest I heard something that I'm not sure I want to mention."

"And what would that have been?"

"I was shopping the other day, Renee and Michael were having a sort of heated conversation in the store. I was at the end of the aisle and they didn't see me."

He took a quick glance in my direction. "Keep going."

"Renee was saying something about how Michael sort of made her come up here against her will. She was saying she would have rather stayed at home. Michael was saying something about trying to keep her safe. Renee seems like a nice lady. You're not thinking she was involved in any way with Michael's murder, are you?"

He kept his gaze straight ahead on the road. "With any investigation, I have to keep an open mind. I haven't ruled out anyone yet, even though Michael was a whistle blower and had a hired gun after him."

"So how is your job going? Ghost tours, right?" He asked changing the subject.

"Yes, it's going pretty good. Some weeks I have more people signed up than others. I may be picking up some business when the bazaar rolls around. I do know I'm apt to get less business as the weather turns colder. No one is going to want to take a ghost tour in the snow."

"Well maybe you could have special snow season ghost tours and offer a hot toddy or cocoa at the end of the tour." He laughed.

I shook my head, "I'm just not sure how well that would go over, but I'll keep your suggestion in mind."

We turned onto the road leading back into town and he asked, "Do you need me to drop you off at your house?"

"No in town is fine, either at the station or the cafe. I'm going to go down and pay Claudette and Renee a visit."

"Your wish is my command." He pulled his car up in front of the cafe, parked and unloaded the two boxes from his back seat, putting them by the cafe door. "Do you need any help getting those in?"

"No. I'm fine. I can get them in. Thanks, I appreciate the ride."

He smiled at me, "Of course. I'll talk to you later." I waved good bye watching him make the short drive back down to the police station. He definitely had a way of making me smile.

CHAPTER TWENTY-NINE

EMILY

ABOUT THE TIME I was getting ready to knock on the cafe door, I looked across the town square and saw Maggie. She appeared to be taking the long way around the square and back to the cafe. I crossed my arms and stared at her as she pulled up in front of the cafe, and got out of the car laughing.

"What? Didn't you have a good ride?"

Still smirking at her I asked, "What are you up to?"

"Oh, come on, I see the way he looks at you. I'm just trying to help things along a bit. He likes you. I know it. You can't tell me you haven't see it too."

"Well whatever the case may be, you need to just leave it alone. We hardly know each other. You know how my last relationship turned out and I'm not sure I'm ready to be in another one just yet."

We knocked on the cafe door and Claudette let us in. "Come on in ladies. Can I get you something?"

"I don't think so, we were just bringing Renee her things."

"Well actually if you ladies have the time, I could maybe use your assistance. I think there is something going on with Renee that we don't know about. Do you have a moment or two to visit with us? She had a couple of rough moments today."

"Sure Claudette" I reassured her, "Whatever you need."

"Let me see if I can get her down here for a cup of tea."

"I'll go put the kettle on and get us a snack if that's ok?"

"Yes please, Emily, thank you. We'll be right back."

Maggie and I trooped off to the kitchen. I put a kettle on and Maggie started looking around to see what was left over to snack on.

"Ooh blueberry scones. What do you think about that?"

"Sounds good to me, I haven't tried one of those yet," I began getting cups as the hibiscus tea was steeping.

We brought the tea and scones out as Claudette returned to the cafe with Renee in tow. "Have a seat, ladies, I think we have everything."

Claudette poured the tea and we passed the scones around. "You know Claudette, I really do need to learn how to make these. They might just be my new favorite." I said after a few bites.

"Renee, we brought your clothes and things back down from the cabin" Maggie said in-between bites.

"Thank you, I really didn't want to go up there. I appreciate you both taking the time to go up there for me."

Claudette looked over at me and Maggie. "Maybe after we finish eating you can bring her things in for her." She then looked over at Renee, "If you don't mind, why don't you let them drive your car around back and park it back there out of sight."

"No problem." Maggie and I must have had a puzzled look on our faces.

Claudette continued on. "It seems like there is someone in town that Renee does not want to see."

"Renee? Is there something you need some help with?" I didn't want to push too hard, she seemed so vulnerable right now.

Renee dropped her head, she sighed heavily and I noticed as she raised her head, she had tears in her eyes. "I think I'm just over reacting. Michael getting killed has me all messed up."

"Well I'd be surprised if it didn't. Losing a spouse is devastating, regardless of what your relationship was like." Oops, maybe I shouldn't have added that last part I thought to myself. I looked up to see the ladies all looking at me with puzzled looks on their faces.

"I'm sorry Renee, but I was in the grocery store." That was all I was going to say.

Renee shook her head, "then you probably heard an earful. I'll admit Michael and I have had some disagreements. Especially recently, I didn't think I needed to be here with him, and you're right I didn't want to come up here with him. He was afraid and didn't want me staying home by myself. He thought I'd be a target."

Claudette set her teacup down and looked over "Well all marriages have trouble from time to time. I'm sure having to go through a pending investigation and going up against a big corporation has made it especially tough on both of you. Is there anything else going one that we can maybe help you with?"

"I suppose you are referring to my disappearance today during work?"

Claudette didn't respond, she was just waiting for an explanation from Renee.

"Not sure what if anything, I actually need you to do. That man that was in here today for lunch, well he's a guy I used to go out with a long time ago. This was way before Michael, and I guess I was just startled to see him."

Claudette looked at Maggie, "You might be interested to know this man is Steven."

Maggie and I were probably both looked surprised.

"What?" Maggie exclaimed. "Steven, the guy that is working on my cabin?"

"Wow, what a small world." I said sipping my tea.

Renee was looking down at her cup of tea, so I ventured on. "So, Renee, seeing him, was this a good thing or a bad thing?"

"Let's just say we didn't part ways amicably."

"How serious is this Renee? Does Detective Mason know?" I didn't mean to be firing questions at her so rapidly.

We all looked at Renee. "No, I'm sure it's nothing. I thought I had seen his truck a few days ago, but I figured what were the odds that he would be in town. I mean, why would he be here? I thought I was imagining things. After all there's got to be a ton of trucks in the area that are like his."

"I'm going to keep Renee close, she can work when she wants and go back upstairs any time she needs to."

Renee made a quick run upstairs to retrieve her keys and handed them over to Maggie.

"I'll go bring your bag in and move the car." Maggie got up and went out the front door. Claudette locked it behind her and went through the kitchen to open the back door.

I stowed the other two boxes in the trunk of her car and Maggie came back in with her bag.

Renee stood up and started clearing the dishes off the table.

"Ok ladies," Maggie said looking at Renee and Claudette, "you stay safe and of course, if there's trouble, call the police."

Renee spoke up, "Really, I'm sure it's nothing."

Maggie and I left and walked down the street together, talking over what we had just learned. "I got the impression that Renee was trying to down play that whole thing. She seems like a pretty straightforward person. Surely she and Steven aren't in this together."

Maggie looked over at me. "What? You think Renee might have had something to do with Michael's murder? Claudette believes in her."

"I'd like to believe Renee, but I think we're missing a piece to this puzzle. Maggie, I don't have a good feeling about this at all. I'm hoping she hasn't pulled the wool over on all of us."

"You don't have a good feeling?" Maggie said, her voice rising, "I hired the guy to work on my cabin. I'm such an idiot. I called and checked his references. He didn't have any dissatisfied customers."

"No, it's not you, Maggie. Some people can project whatever facade they want to. I think I'll pay a visit to Detective Mason tomorrow and bring him up to date on this. I think he should know, and besides, the autopsy results should be back by then too. Who knows what I can find out."

"I think I agree with you." Maggie admitted

"I'll keep you updated. After I see Detective Mason

tomorrow, I'll stop by the shop and let you know what he said."

"You want to do dinner?"

"No, I can't tomorrow, I have a tour booked. Only one guest tomorrow night, but a booking is a booking." We said our good-byes and parted ways. My mind was spinning, full of questions.

CHAPTER THIRTY

EMILY

I CALLED and made an appointment to meet with Detective Mason late in the afternoon. I figured I could meet with him, stop by and update Maggie, and then make it to the Gage Hotel to start my tour. I swung by the coffee shop and picked up two caramel lattes. Might as well try to butter up the detective and see if it would prove helpful in obtaining information. As I entered the police station, Detective Mason met me.

"Hope you're not tired of caramel." I held the cup out to him.

He took the cup from me and ushered me into a conference room. "Thank you, I love any kind of coffee anytime. This stuff is so much better that what we make here." He laughed, indicating a seat. "So, what can I do for you? Is everything going ok with Claudette?"

"Yes and no. I mean Claudette is fine. And Renee is doing okay helping out over there. But here is the problem.

There was a man in the cafe, who seems to have spooked Renee."

"Did Renee tell Claudette what was going on? Who was the man? Do we have a description or anything?"

"Well, I'm not sure of all the specifics, but I do think Renee is holding back. In fact, I think she was down playing the seriousness. And yes, I know who the man is."

"Who, is he?"

"Steven, the man who is doing work on Maggie's cabin. Maggie said she had reached out to his former clients before she hired him and they were happy with his work, but that doesn't mean much."

"Do you have a last name for him?"

"I knew you were going to ask me that. Honestly, I can't remember it now, but Maggie has it though. I'm sure she can give you whatever information she has on him."

"Okay, I'll give her a call or if you happen to see her, have her stop by."

"I'd be happy to, in fact I told her I'd come to see her right after I left here. We just thought you ought to know. You don't suppose that Renee and this guy Steven were involved in this together do you. Surely, she's not putting on some kind of act in front of Claudette. I'd hate to see Claudette get hurt in any way, she's a really special lady."

He rubbed his chin, "These are all things I have to consider as a detective. Thanks Emily. I appreciate the new info."

"Speaking of info, by any chance is the autopsy report back yet?"

He gave me a quizzical look. "As a matter of fact, it is, but Emily you know this is a police matter. I can't be sharing this information with you?

"Oh, come on, you know I have a knack for figuring

things out. And by the way, I'm sharing information with you. I can help, I know I can."

He gave me a big smile. "Thank you for the latte." He stood up and walked me out of the police station. I started down the sidewalk on my way to see Maggie, then turned around to see him smiling at me. He lifted his hand and gave me a little wave good bye.

CHAPTER THIRTY-ONE

EMILY

"HEY MAGGIE" I called walking into her shop. At least I noticed there was no customers in the shop before I called out for her. Like so many times before she came out from the back room where she was working on arrangements.

"Hey. So, did you find anything out from Detective Mason?"

"He wants you to go by the station when you have time and if you can bring him Steven's business card or whatever you have on him."

"Sure, glad to help in any way I can. I really want to find out what's going on."

"Detective Mason told me the autopsy results were back. He wouldn't give me any specifics though. I sure would like to get an actual look at the report, but not sure how I'm going to lay my hands on it. Last time I got a peek at an autopsy report was only because he left it on his desk and no one else was around. I'm not sure I will get that lucky again." She was putting the finishing touches on an arrangement of sunflowers, orange gerbera daisies and mums, possible only half listening. "So, you say you want to find out what is going on?"

"Definitely, I hope Detective Mason goes up there and gets to the bottom of things."

About that time her phone rang. I watched and listened to her side of the conversation.

"Hello. Uh-huh, okay I think I can do that. Okay see you tomorrow." She hung up the phone, with a reluctant look on her face.

"What's up?"

"That was Steven. He said he's almost finished and wondered if I wanted to come up and check out the cabin."

"He's pretty fast. That didn't seem to take him too long. What's the hesitation? I can go with you if you like."

"Would you mind? I know it's probably ridiculous, but I'm a little nervous to be around him now."

"Of course not, happy to. I hope he did a good job. If he's as fast with the other cabins, then you could definitely get them available for summer renting. That'd be awesome." I was obviously more excited about the situation than she was.

"How about tomorrow? Are you free? I can try to get someone in to watch the shop for me. I'll get back with you on the time, if that's okay.

"Sounds like a plan." The rest of the afternoon was fairly quiet at the shop. She finished up with the one arrangement and we enjoyed visiting with each other while we tidied up the back room.

After a while I looked at my watch, "Okay, time for me

to go." I grabbed my light jacket. "I need to go meet my tour. We'll talk tomorrow?"

"Yes, and I'll make sure Detective Mason gets the business card and I'll provide him a list his references I called too."

"Ok sounds good. Call me tomorrow."

CHAPTER THIRTY-TWO

EMILY

I WALKED on down street to the Gage Hotel. I was still a few minutes early, so I took a seat on one of the wrought iron benches right outside of the hotel entrance. I pulled out my phone to check my email. There were no new emails, so someone was going to get a private ghost tour tonight. The late afternoon light was fading fast as the days were getting shorter. It was going to be a clear night tonight and would make for a good tour. The slight breeze carried the fragrance of the clematis blossoms that were growing in the hotel garden. I continued scrolling through my emails while I waited. After a moment I looked up and saw a familiar figure coming across the square. I waved at Detective Mason, just a hello in passing sort of wave and continued with what I was doing. When I looked back up I couldn't help but notice he was coming in my direction. My heart gave a little flutter and I silently chided myself for getting excited. I stood up sliding my phone in my back jeans pocket and watched as he approached.

"Good evening Emily. I hope I'm not too late."

"Excuse me?"

"I have a tour tonight" he pulled out a printed confirmation from his pocket. "Do you need this?"

"No of course not." I was trying to control the smile on my face. "Whatever made you want to take my tour?"

"Well for all the time I've lived here, I had no idea we had anything haunted in Copper Ridge. I thought it would be a good idea to learn more about my town and see how much I actually believe that anything here could be haunted." His dark eyes sparkled as he smiled at me.

"Well then why don't we get started."

"Is there anyone else coming tonight? Do we need to wait?"

"No, sir. Tonight, you will have a private tour."

It could have been my imagination, but I thought his smile got a little bigger. I turned, unable to keep the smile off my face.

Detective Mason followed me down closer to the sidewalk, we turned to face the Gage Hotel. "I relayed the history of the building of the hotel and then launched into the ghost story. A few years after the hotel originally opened, there was a man who suffered a terrible injury right outside the hotel. He was crossing the road when he was run down by a team of runaway horses." I walked him into the hotel and stopped in the lobby to continue my story.

"The victim was brought inside, and placed in a room right down that hallway." Detective Mason turned to look. "The town doctor was summoned, but unfortunately, his injuries were too severe and he died later that day. As the story goes, the man was coming into the hotel to meet his soon to be bride who was waiting for him here. Since then, hotel guests have seen a young man, dressed in a suit, holding his rounded derby hat, walking through the halls. His hair is freshly cut and combed and his mustache is waxed. Whenever anyone tries to follow him, he disappears around a corner and is gone. He appears to be walking the halls, possibly searching for his bride. The man who died was none other than Mr. Gage, owner of the Gage Hotel. He was on his way back to his hotel for his wedding. His bride was heartbroken and soon returned to her family back east. He has been in the hotel searching for her ever since."

"Phew, one guy saved from the bonds of matrimony." He said with a laugh.

I was a little surprised by his comment. He never came across as the cynical kind. The words escaped my mouth before I could stop them. "You don't believe in marriage?"

"That sounded bad didn't it? Let's just say, it's going to take someone really special to make me think about marriage." He gave me a playful grin, "Maybe I just haven't met the right someone yet."

The last part of his statement caught me a little off guard, but I answered quickly, "Then again, maybe you have."

I turned and headed to the hotel's front doors, slightly mortified. I wasn't usually so bold. I couldn't believe I had actually said that. Why couldn't I have just kept my mouth shut? It didn't take long, he caught up with me. There was a smile on his face as he opened the door for me.

We left the hotel walked on through the square, we stopped at the court house and I gave him the history of both the court house and the old stone jail. We walked on down and approached Evergreen Manor.

"I'm sure you know; this is Evergreen Manor. This

four-story Victorian manor was built in the mid 1800s by the local railroad tycoon. Mr. Armstrong moved his wife and family in. Later, a flu epidemic swept through town. Mrs. Armstrong cared for her husband and twin girls around the clock. Unfortunately, all three ended up passing away.

"I've heard a little bit about this family's history. It was awful."

"You're right, because not only did Mrs. Armstrong lose her husband and daughters, she also ended up losing her new baby. The story says she was a strong and sturdy woman, but the long hours, hard work and exposure to her sick family, finally took its toll. She fell ill, which left the maid to care for her and the young baby. The maid was becoming sick herself, tripped, and fell down one of the staircases in the house while carrying the baby. Both the baby and maid were killed in the fall. Mrs. Armstrong recovered, but she was the only one in her family to survive. As the story goes, she was never the same after that. Her whole family was gone. She lived out her life in solitude. It's said that lights can be seen in the windows late at night, especially in the fourth-floor nursery. It could be Mrs. Armstrong wandering around the house crying over the loss of her precious family. Have you ever seen any lights on at night?" I asked?

"No, but now I'm going to have to watch for them." He said looking up at the house. "I wonder if it could be kids breaking in there? I'm going to have to go back now and make sure everything is locked up tight. I hear the last owner died and I think the heirs are trying to decide what to do with the property."

"It really is a gorgeous house. It's a shame that it's empty." I replied, gazing up at the beautiful structure.

He looked back at me, "Well, if your tours go well, maybe you can buy it."

I laughed, "Twenty rooms, it's a bit big for just me. No, it needs a family." We continued on and eventually came to our next stop.

"As you may know, this is the Carriage House. It is a three-story Victorian home, which was originally owned by the town banker. He and his family had moved to town and had the house custom built. Many of the furnishings were shipped in from back east. That beautiful stained glass rose window up there was made and shipped over from Italy. The family loved to host elaborate parties."

"Want to hear something funny?" the detective asked me.

"Sure."

"When I was about six or seven years old this house was vacant and I threw a rock at that window. Of course, from where I was standing the rock didn't even hit the house. My momma saw me and let's just say I never tried that ever again." He paused for a moment still gazing up at the window. "As I got older I began to appreciate how pretty it was. I'm glad it's survived all these years."

"It is pretty isn't it? And I'm really glad you weren't older when you tried that stunt, you might have actually hit it."

"So, who is supposedly haunting this place?" He asked as he nodded toward the carriage house.

"According to history, after the family had died, the home was used for many different things - a boarding house, a temporary stop over for small troop movements, an office building, and even a brothel. Of course, you know now it has been purchased, restored and opened as a Bed & Breakfast. Some guests who have stayed there have reported hearing things. From what I have been told they hear what sounds like a party, music, people talking and laughing and the sounds of glasses clinking together." I smiled up at him. "It seems the banker and his family are pleased with the restoration and are again hosting their parties."

"Huh," detective Mason asked, " I wonder how the owners are taking it? I mean, some people might not appreciate living somewhere that is potentially haunted. Not to mention of how it might affect their business."

"I hear they are taking it all in stride. As far as I know they aren't advertising it as haunted. But if they did, I'm sure they may get more guests who come in hopes of seeing or hearing something."

We left the Carriage House, walked up the road and then up the hill to the old Copper Ridge Cemetery.

"Well now I shouldn't be surprised we ended up here."

I laughed looking up at him, "It's ok Detective, I haven't lost a guest to a ghost yet. I'm sure you know this cemetery was the first one the town ever had. The graves date back into the 1800s. A lot of the head stones are so worn that you can barely read the names and dates. There were stories about mining accidents that occurred back in the day and some of the miners who died in those accidents are buried here. There are some reports of people seeing floating orbs of light, possibly the ghosts of miners carrying their lamps, possibly looking for fellow miners that have been lost to the mine. Feel free to walk through the cemetery and look around at anything you like."

He started to walk off, "Want to come with me."

We walked together through the oldest section of the cemetery. Detective Mason stopped to examine some of the oldest headstones.

"There is so much history here," he said as he stood

looking at the headstone of one of the town founders. You know I've never come up here. I might need to read up on our town's history. Thank you. I've enjoyed this."

We turned, headed out of the cemetery and started walking back into town. I stopped and turned to look up at the mountain. "Mrs. Smithers told me about stories of lights appearing up on the mountain. She found old journal entries from the mine owner. They talk about miners seeing lights in the woods. Maggie and I are going to go up the mountain to investigate, but we just haven't had time yet."

"And maybe that's a good thing. For now, until this murder is solved, you and Maggie need to stay off the mountain, especially after dark," he turned and looked at me. "Tell me you understand, this is serious."

"I understand. No going up the mountain after dark, until the murder is solved." I recite his comments back to him. We continued our walk back to the hotel, taking our time. He was surprisingly easy to talk to. All too soon we were standing outside the Gage Hotel. "Well Detective, I hope you have enjoyed your tour tonight. Here is your drink ticket courtesy of the new owners of the hotel."

"Why thank you. As a matter of fact, I have had a very pleasant evening." His eyes really did sparkle when he smiled. "Thank you for the tour. I don't believe in ghosts, but I did have fun. Why don't you come in with me and we can get a drink, maybe talk some more, unless you need to go?"

I smiled up at him. "I'd love to Detective, thank you."

"You know you could call me Alex." He said with a smile.

We walked into the hotel bar, ordered our drinks and got a table together. Maggie would be grinning wildly if she knew we were having a drink together. I tried to tell myself, it was just a drink, not a big deal. "So, I talked to Maggie this afternoon. She said she'd stop by to see you in the morning to drop off the information she has on Steven. I don't know what the deal is with him and Renee, but I hope for Maggie's sake that he is legit. Maybe that is selfish, but I'd like her to be able to get her cabin completed without any drama. She and I are supposed to stop by the cabin that Steven's working on tomorrow. He called and asked her to come check it out.

He sputtered a little. "Didn't we just have this conversation? No! No going up there."

"You said after dark. We won't be up there after dark." I tried looking at him with a straight face. "I promise that we will go during the day and just check on her cabin. How does that sound?"

"Honestly I don't know. I haven't had a chance to speak with this guy yet. We don't know what is going on with him."

"But don't we think this was just a company trying to get rid of a whistle blower?"

"That's definitely what it seems like."

"Well if that's the case, do you really think the killer would be hanging around town. No, they would shoot and then go. There would be no reason for them to be hanging around."

Detective Mason looked down at his drink and sighed loudly. "Look, I can't make you do anything, just promise me you and Maggie will be careful. If you do feel like you have to go up there, then stick together and whatever you do, don't say anything about Renee. If Michael's murder really was a company sort of "hit", then the killer is probably long gone. I agree with you, no one would stick around a town after they have killed someone. Either way I have guys searching the local hotels for anyone suspicious or who doesn't seem to have legitimate business. Anyway, just be careful."

"I will and I certainly wouldn't say anything about Renee."

"Yes, and can you not poke your nose around anywhere you shouldn't?"

"Of course, I can." I smiled weakly, wondering if he could see what I was actually thinking, which was how much I really wanted to get a look at the full police report and the results of the autopsy.

"You know I can think of other things I'd rather talk about than this murder." He said with one of his dazzling smiles, "like how did you end up in Copper Ridge?"

I gave him the Cliff notes version, which reminded me of how much I missed my mother.

He reached over and took my hand, "I'm sorry for your loss, Emily. I'm sorry if I stirred up any painful memories."

He let my hand go after only a few seconds, but his touch lingered on my skin. "No, it's okay. She was a sweetie and I cherish my memories of her." I paused for a moment. "Moving to Copper Ridge was a good thing for me and I'm enjoying my ghost tour business.

We continued to enjoy our evening, talking easily. Our drinks had been long since finished when we decided to leave. I felt his hand at the small of my back as we walked out of the hotel together. Again, he dropped his hand the minute we were out the door. I looked up. It was a gorgeous clear night with thousands of stars shining.

"Can I give you a lift home?" He asked when we got to the sidewalk.

"No, that's okay, I have my car. I've had a good

evening." I was thinking this was one of my favorite tours that I had given so far.

"I can say the same. Thank you for the tour and the company."

He walked me to my car and said good night again. I couldn't help but smile all the way home. I kept telling myself it was a tour and a follow up drink. No big deal. But the memory of our time together brought a smile to my face each time I thought of it.

CHAPTER THIRTY-THREE

EMILY

I HAD A MESSAGE FROM MAGGIE, she asked me to stop by her shop the next morning.

"Hey, good timing. She said gathering up some papers. "I was just getting ready to go see Detective Mason and drop off the info I have on Steven."

"Have you had any coffee? I was thinking about going and picking us up a latte or something. Want one?"

"Yeah if you don't mind, that would be great. I'll go drop these papers off and I'll meet you at the police station. How does that sound?"

"See you there." I walked down to the coffee shop, enjoying the cool crisp air and the morning sunshine. I placed my order and smiled as I thought about ordering one for Detective Mason too. With my drink tray in hand I walked back down to the police station. Detective Mason and Maggie were just coming out from the back and into the lobby.

"So, did you fork over all your stuff on Steven?" I asked holding out her coffee.

"Sure did, thanks." Maggie said taking her cup from me.

"And this one is for you." I held out the latte to Detective Mason. Alex, I thought to myself smiling.

"Why thank you." He smiled taking his latte. "This is becoming a habit" he laughed, "actually one that I could get used to."

I couldn't help but smile. Maggie seemed to be standing there just taking it all in.

"Okay, Maggie, are you ready?" I turned to her, hoping my face wasn't too red.

"Goodbye Detective." I turned to leave, with Maggie following. We stepped outside and I continued walking down the sidewalk. I could feel Maggie's eyes on me and I tried to ignore her. Finally, when I couldn't ignore her any longer, I stopped walking and turned to look at her. "What?"

"Am I seeing some sparks between you two?" she asked with a big grin on her face.

"I don't know what you are talking about."

"You're blushing." She laughed

"Don't be ridiculous. It's nothing." I knew I was a little self-conscious about the exchange Alex and I had, mostly because we had an audience. "Now are you coming with me or not?"

Maggie laughed. "Are you trying to change the subject?"

"I don't know what you're talking about. Aren't you excited to see how your first cabin turned out."

"I'm not sure which I'm more excited about, my cabin or your love life." Maggie was having fun teasing me.

I shook my head and continued down the sidewalk

sipping my latte. Maggie caught up with me and we piled in her car and made our way leisurely up the mountain. The forest was absolutely gorgeous this time of year, a mixture of orange, yellow and red. "It really is beautiful up here. I can't get over how pretty it is."

"You're right, it is. You know, living here, it's really easy to just take it for granted. I've lived here for so long, it's nice to see this through someone else's eyes."

We pulled onto the road that ran up to the cabin. She slowed her car. Steven's red pick-up was in the driveway.

"Ok, so if you go inside and keep Steven occupied, I'll have chance to look in his truck. When I finish, I'll come inside."

Maggie looked at me like I had two heads. "What are you talking about?"

"I'm going to take a quick peek in his truck."

"Why?"

"I'm just going to see if he has anything out of the ordinary there."

"Are you crazy? You can't do that."

"Just keep him busy inside for a few minutes. You can get him to show you all of his repair work."

"What do I do if he doesn't stay inside? I'm not sure I can do this." Maggie was beginning to sweat.

"Look, just do the best you can. I have faith in you. And if he starts to come out, just call my name real loud and act like I've gone down to the lake or something."

I slumped way down in my seat, while Maggie pulled her car up to the cabin and parked behind Steven's truck. She got out of the car as Steven came around the side of the cabin. I scooted lower in my seat and listened carefully to the conversation.

"Hey Steven, thanks for calling me. I can't wait to see how things have turned out."

"Glad you could come by so soon. I've made good progress, I think you're going to like it. Here let me show you."

Their footsteps crunching on the gravel retreated into the distance. I raised my head just a bit and took a quick glance. Steven had just rounded the side of the cabin with Maggie following. She took a quick glance back at me. As soon as she rounded the corner, I eased the car door open. I kept my eyes on the corner of the cabin, it was a good thing none of the cabin windows faced the driveway where we were parked. The interior light came on as I eased the pickup door open. I wasn't certain exactly what I was expecting to find, but I'd know it when I saw it. There wasn't anything out of the ordinary in the center console. I peeked under the passenger seat next, where there was what appeared to be a lady's blouse. That's odd. I slide it back in place and opened the glove box and pulled out an envelope. It contained photos, lots of photos, of Renee. Could she really be involved with Steven? I kept thumbing through the photos, the location in the backgrounds didn't look familiar, I had to assume they were taken in the town she was from. I flipped through a few more and saw photos of Renee and Michael, and some photos of just Michael. Why would Steven have these pictures?

About that time, I heard Maggie talking louder than normal, "So the deck sure looks nice. If we thinned the trees just a little it would have a lovely view of the lake."

I shut the truck door as quietly as possible and started back toward the car. I stopped in my tracks when I heard Steven call out, "Hey what are you doing, messing in my truck?"

My heart started racing. What was I going to do? Act normal, I told myself. I suddenly realized I still had the pack of photos in my hand. I quickly slid the packet of photos in the waist band of my jeans and pulled my shirt down. I turned around and held my phone pretending to be talking to someone.

"Hold on I said into my phone. I faced Steven. "You must be Steven I said holding out my hand. Sorry, didn't mean anything, I was just looking for paper and a pen."

He scowled at me and didn't shake my hand. I didn't think he was buying my explanation. Maggie came up behind him and started talking rapidly.

"Steven, this is my friend Emily, she was accompanying me today. I'm sure she didn't mean any harm."

Steven stepped up to the truck and wrenched open the passenger side door. He reached in to open the glove box and I knew we were in trouble.

"Where is it?"

I knew exactly what he meant and we were caught. But I still tried to bluff. "Where is what?"

"Give them back now!" he clenched his jaw.

I didn't know what to do except comply. I reached up and pulled the envelope from my waist band and he snatched it from me. Maggie looked scared and puzzled all at the same time.

"You need to leave." This comment seemed to bring Maggie to life.

"Hey now, wait a minute, this is my property," her voice taking on an authoritative tone.

"She stole this from my truck." Steven was holding the packet of photos up and glaring at Maggie.

"Well now you have it back." A deep baritone voice

startled all of us. I turned to see Detective Mason standing down the drive way.

"He has photos of Renee and Michael, a lot of them. There is even one photo with an X through Michael's face." I was talking rapidly and my heart was pounding.

About that time Steven reached in his tool belt and pulled out his hammer holding it high. "You don't understand, she is mine. He had no right to her. I was her perfect match, she should be with me and now that he's gone, she can be mine."

Detective Mason had pulled his gun, aiming it at Steven. Maggie had backed up and rounded the pickup to get out of the way, but unfortunately, I was still right in the line of fire. My eyes darting back and forth between his face and the hammer. I started backing up as slowly as possible.

"He wasn't good for her. He put her in danger, dragging her up here to hide out like a criminal." Stevens face was turning red with veins bulging at his temples.

"So, you killed him. You hit him, didn't you? You hit him with that hammer? I'm sure if we test it, we'll find traces of Michaels blood on it." Detective Mason was slowing advancing on Steven.

"He wasn't good enough for her. Yes, I killed him. Now that he's gone, we can be together. She'll realize that I am the one she wants, not him!" By now he was screaming. "She'll see, she'll be better off with me."

I had managed to back up a few more steps during his rant. I suddenly threw myself to the ground behind his truck which let Detective Mason do his thing.

"Drop the hammer." He yelled.

Steven paused holding the hammer high. He seemed to realize that it was over, and lowered his arm dropping the hammer. Detective Mason hurried to kick the hammer away. I could hear Detective Mason reading him his rights as he put him in handcuffs. He led him back to his car, and secured him in the back seat. Maggie and I huddled together on the other side of his truck, just trying to stay down and out of the way.

"It's clear ladies."

We stood up, still holding onto each other. Detective Mason had the envelope of photos. "Are you ladies ok? Right after you left the police station I received a report on Steven. Renee has a restraining order out on him. I knew you were coming up here, so I tried to get up here as fast as I could."

"We're good" I reassured him.

"Or we will be." Maggie stammered. "I'm so sorry Emily, I tried to keep him in the cabin I really did."

"Shh, Maggie, it's ok. I shouldn't have involved you."

"I don't think either of you should have taken this on by yourself. You know that's what the police are for. I'm just glad I got here in time. Are you doing okay? Do you think you can make it back to the station by yourself?"

"Yes, sure. We're good, thank you." Maggie gave me her keys and asked me to drive, so she could pull herself together." I looked over at her as I got ready to start the car up. "Maggie, I'm really sorry I got you involved." She gave me a shaky smile.

"Let's get back to town, I need some tea or coffee and some sugar to offset my stress."

I drove back to town to The Little Copper I and we got ourselves a table. When Claudette and Renee had a moment, we told them of our experiences. Renee plunked herself down in a chair at our table, her face white. The cafe was still open for business and I could tell she was trying to hold herself together.

"Why don't you go on back upstairs and lay down." Claudette said, patting her on the shoulder.

"No. I'm not going to let him rule my life. He has taken away enough from me already. I know there will be time to mourn for Michael, but for now I have a job to do." Renee stood back up, smoothed her clothes, and looked at Claudette. She tilted her head back, "Come on Claudette, we have work to do."

"I'll bring you ladies some tea and scones. Just sit right there," Claudette said.

"Thanks Claudette" we both said at the same time.

"Wow, I'm not so sure I would be holding up so well," Maggie said shaking her head.

"I don't think she'll be so brave for long, but for now, I guess she is doing what she thinks she needs to."

CHAPTER THIRTY-FOUR

EMILY

A COUPLE OF DAYS LATER, Renee, Maggie, Claudette and I sat in the cafe, enjoying a late afternoon cup of tea and treats. We had given our reports to Detective Mason. Renee had been in the station and relayed her story in detail. It seems that Steven had not taken their break up well even though it had been years ago. He turned into a full-blown stalker. It had even gotten worse after she and Michael married. He had become obsessed with her and would sit in his truck outside her home, and come into her salon. She and Michael had moved and Renee had changed jobs, all in an attempt to avoid him. Steven had subsequently tracked her down, and even started to make threats to Michael. Eventually they had taken out the restraining order and for a while it looked like it was working.

Detective Mason had let us know there was a man in town that had also been looking for Michael. He heard this from the prosecutor. He had even tracked him down to a local hotel. After Michael was killed, the man's car broke down and one of the mechanics at a local garage had worked on it. By the time the detective showed up he had hit the road.

Claudette had bought out a spread of scones, her famous orange cranberry bread and her new spicy pumpkin muffins.

"Try these ladies. It's almost that time of year for me to make all things pumpkin."

"Oh, wow Claudette, these are great." I tried not talking with my mouth full.

We all had a good time together, eating and chatting together.

"Renee, we sure are going to miss you here." Maggie smiled at her.

"I certainly know I am" Claudette chimed in. "I know you probably wouldn't want a job as a waitress, but there is always one here for you, if you ever need it."

Renee reached over to take Claudette's hand. "I can't begin to thank you for taking me in." And ladies, thank you for helping to solve Michael's murder. I don't know how I could have made it through this time without your help. For now, I have a job to get back to, but who knows. Maybe one of these days if I get tired of the big city I could head back this way and open up a salon here."

We finished up our treats and helped Renee load her car. We said our goodbyes and watched her drive off.

Claudette turned to us, "Are you ladies ready to get back to planning for the Fall Bazaar?"

We both laughed, "Yes I guess we are. Lead on Claudette, let's get to work."

NOTES FROM THE AUTHOR

Thank you so much for reading my second Cozy Mystery. My hope is that you will stick with me throughout the series. I have enjoyed writing these stories and watching my characters develop over the course of these books. I hope you enjoy them.

Other books in the series include:
    Murder Down the Hill
    Murder in the Square
    Murder Down the Stairs
    Murder on the Stage
    Murder Down the Aisle
    Murder at the Shelter
    Murder to Go
    Murder on the River
    Murder at the Manor

If you would like to receive my newsletter and get information on future books, please go to my website at www.amygrundy.com

Again, thank you for reading this book, I sincerely hope you enjoyed it. Here is a preview of Book Three in this series:

PREVIEW OF BOOK 3 - MURDER IN THE SQUARE

Chapter 1

I woke up with the pale morning sun streaming through my bedroom window. I pulled the blanket up around my head and rolled over. I had been looking forward to today, which was the start of the Copper Ridge Fall Bazaar, but as I lay there, I realized I had a sense of foreboding. My name is Emily Rose, and I was fairly new in town, having moved here about five months ago. My move here had taken a leap of faith following the death of my beloved mother and the crash and burn of my relationship with my boyfriend. Mom had left me a modest inheritance and I moved to Copper Ridge to start my new business.

As crazy as it might sound to some, I had always wanted to have a ghost tour business, and now my dream had come to pass. I wasn't really sure I believed in ghosts, but I enjoyed meeting new people and weaving stories in this old historic town. I pushed aside all thoughts of my old flame and my old life, heaved the covers aside and climbed out of bed. I dressed comfortably today, because I knew I'd be running around and assisting with the setup for the bazaar. I threw on my jeans, sneakers, and a long sleeve Henley, then grabbed my favorite pullover hoodie. I was almost out the door, when I stopped to swipe on some sunscreen to protect my fair complexion, and shoved a lip balm in my pocket.

I ran out the door, pushing back the uneasy feeling in the pit of my stomach. A short drive later, I pulled my little car up in front of The Little Copper Cafe. I rushed up, and knocked on the door. It had been temporarily closed this morning in preparation for the opening of the bazaar. Claudette unlocked the door and welcomed me in.

"Sorry, I know I'm late, just couldn't seem to get it together this morning."

"You're not too late, and trust me when I say we're all going to have plenty to do today. Here, have a seat and let me get you some coffee." Claudette bustled off to get the coffee.

I thought to myself, hopefully she'd bring me some of her goodies to go with it.

"Hey girlie, you look a little troubled this morning. What's up?" Maggie, my best friend in town, was sitting there enjoying an enormous blueberry muffin. It was one of Claudette's specialties, the kind with the sweet crumb topping.

"I don't know, just woke up with this weird feeling and I can't seem to shake it."

"Well you know I'm here for you anytime, but today, you won't have time for any weird feelings. Claudette's right, we have a ton of work to do this morning." Maggie said as she picked up her coffee cup.

"Here you go, my dear, you look like you need this," Claudette set down a cup of coffee and a plate with a blueberry muffin and a brown sugar cinnamon scone. "Wasn't sure which you would prefer, so I just brought both," she laughed.

Claudette took her seat at the table, setting down her cup of coffee and her clipboard.

"Okay ladies, most of the big arrangements are already taken care of." She had her pen, checking items off her list, "Lights have been set up in the square, the banners of course have been up for some time now. Tables will to be delivered shortly out in the square. If you can show them where they need to be, that would be great. Joe has had his grills and smokers going all night. They will bring in their gear shortly. The small stage was assembled last night.

Maggie looked at me, "I loved the bands we had last year, I think you're really going to like them."

Claudette spoke up, "Maggie's right, and we've got some of the same ones back this year. They'll be performing throughout the day, it's a lot of fun, sitting out there listening to them. We're going to have some good barbecue today too. I can't wait." Claudette grinned at both of us as she set her clipboard aside.

"Wow, sounds like it's going to be quite the event." This was going to be my first experience at the yearly Copper Ridge Fall Bazaar.

"It is," Maggie said in-between bites of her muffin.

"Besides kicking off our holiday shopping season, and it's just a lot of fun. Everyone in town comes out, and people have a chance to just sit and visit while enjoying some good food and good music too." Claudette had been on the Fall Bazaar committee for several years now. She seemed to have everything in order.

"Okay, let me fuel up and I'll be happy to help out with anything you need today."

I enjoyed my coffee and savored my last bite of my brown sugar cinnamon scone. No one baked like Claudette, and so far, there wasn't anything that she made that I didn't like. Claudette had a curvy figure and soft brown hair. She had been so welcoming and supportive of me after I moved to town.

Claudette laughed. I opened my eyes, looking at her.

"What?"

"I have never seen anyone who seems to enjoy food like you do."

"What can I say, I like to eat good food. I think it's my new hobby," I laughed. For the first time that day, my sense of foreboding seemed to disappear.

"Ok, I'm ready." Maggie stood up and looked at me, "Ready to help get some tables set up?"

"I'm with you." I pushed my chair back, took one last sip of coffee, stood up, and left the cafe. My thoughts about today were brightening up. It was going to be a good day after all. Or at least I thought it was.

Chapter 2

"Good morning, Jessica," Susan entered Jessica's jewelry shop called "Silver Creations". She had a big grin on her face. "Today's going to be a great day, I can just feel it. Am I too early?"

Jessica gave a shrug, "Nope, you're the first one here. Everyone else should be here anytime now."

Susan was a young local artist in Copper Ridge who specialized in beautiful stained-glass pieces. About that time the little bell over the door tinkled; they both turned as Randy and Teresa came in together. Randy was a local artist who also dabbled in sculpting. Teresa specialized in jewelry making like Jessica.

Randy took a quick look around the shop, "So guess he's not here yet." Randy huffed. "I don't know about you ladies, but I'm not so sure we're getting a good deal with this guy. I wish I had never signed that contract."

"It's boosted my business, that's for sure," Susan piped up.

Jessica hopped up to refill her coffee cup. "Well, let's see how the reports look and see what new contacts Larry has for us."

"We have another six months on our contracts," Randy still did not seem too happy. "Guess I can't do anything until it expires anyway."

The little bell jangled again and a middle-aged man wearing black framed glasses and a gray suit came through the door. He seemed to carry with him an air of smug importance. "Good morning, all. So, what's going on out there?" He turned, looking back out the window.

"Good morning, Mr. Jacobson. Today's our annual fall bazaar. It's sort of the kickoff to our holiday shopping season. You should stick around and enjoy the festivities. They're going to be serving up some world-class BBQ later today." Susan was the most welcoming of the group, chatting easily with him as she stood to extend her hand to him.

"Now Susan, you know you can call me Larry," he said, shaking her hand and giving her a big smile. He seemed to come across to some as a slick, smooth talking kind of guy but Susan didn't seem to notice.

"Can I get you a cup of coffee, Mr. Jacobson?" Teresa asked, making her way to the coffeepot.

"Yes, if you don't mind, with sugar and cream too."

Mr. Jacobson drew up a chair on one side of Jessica's worn work table. He snapped open his briefcase, bringing out the much-anticipated reports. "I know you've all been waiting for these." The reports contained specifics for each business and he had copies for each of them. The four businesses had formed a co-op of sorts and had hired Mr. Jacobson to help each shop network and expand their businesses. He would locate other shops in bigger cities that were willing to sell their jewelry or art. It sounded like a really good idea when he first approached them. He seemed to know what he was talking about and he was able to provide information of other businesses he had helped. It obviously provided a much better opportunity to get their products seen by more people, which at the time seemed like a really good idea. The down side? Mr. Jacobson took a cut, and some of the shop owners didn't think they were making enough in return.

"As you can see, each report shows which shops and galleries your products are in currently and how much is selling in each location. Toward the back of the packet, you will see a list of proposed shops that we could include in the future if you would like additional expansion. As I see it, this is a win-win opportunity for me, and all of your little businesses."

"Of course, we can't get spread too thin, we have to be able to keep up with the demand, so to speak," Theresa mentioned hesitantly. She, like Randy, wasn't exactly sold on the current arrangement.

Mr. Jacobson sat there with his hands folded on his over-sized middle. "Why don't you take your time, look the reports over. I'll be in town for a couple of days, I can stop by and speak with you individually, and we can figure out what you'd like to do in the future."

"Sounds like a plan to me," Jessica chimed in. Jessica

and Susan were a little more open to continuing their current arrangement.

"Then it's settled." Mr. Jacobson stood up, snapped his briefcase closed and walked out without allowing for any further discussion. The little copper bell jangled in his wake.

Randy was browsing through the reports with a scowl on his face. "Well I don't know about you guys, but I want out of this deal, any way I can. He's got my stuff in crappy places and so far, I'm paying him to do it. He's running a racket and I fell for it. This is just a total rip-off." Randy got up, scraping his chair on the old wooden floors, and stomped off, leaving the ladies speechless.

Teresa flipped her packet closed and sighed, "Guess we best get going, hopefully today will be a profitable day for all of us."

"We can hope." They all agreed, and said their good-byes, Susan and Teresa leaving to get their own shops ready to open for the day.

Chapter 3

"Geez, I'm beat." I plunked down on a park bench beside Maggie. "So far, I have helped set up some additional booths, and get tables and chairs put up in the little kids' section. Who knew you guys would have so much to see and do today?"

"Yep, can you see why we only do this sort of thing once a year? Although there has been talk about another festival in the late spring. The city council is still talking about it."

"Suppose it's good for the town's economy."

"Yes, but more than that, it's an opportunity for the people here to come out and have some fun. The high school art department sets up in the kids' section; and they offer face painting for the kids and a couple of different crafts. There's also a couple who make balloon animals. The kids really love it." Maggie's sunny personality was showing and I sure didn't want to bring her down. She was genuinely enthusiastic about the event. I nodded as she continued to talk.

"Besides the actual shops, the booths that you helped set up are filled with locals who come out to sell products. You'll see, they'll be filled with everything from wood carvings to homemade soap, pickles, and all kinds of fudge. You have got to stop by and get some of the fudge. My favorite is the peanut butter. There is a lady in town named Dorothy Johnston; no one makes peanut butter fudge like she does. It's really incredible. Anyway, now that it's all set up, you can enjoy it."

"I think I'll just sit here for a little bit." I answered.

"Why don't I go get us some lattes and you can catch your second wind."

"I'll never turn down a latte, thanks."

"Peppermint mocha or pumpkin spice?" Maggie asked.

"Surprise me."

Maggie hopped up off the bench. I watched her setting off at a clip that would make a jackrabbit jealous. My gosh, where did that woman get her energy? I shook my head, and smiled as I sat there. It was nice sitting here, it gave me an opportunity to enjoy the weather and at least try to relax. It was beautiful outside this time of year. They couldn't have picked a better day for an outside event. A slight wind rustled through the leaves of the maple and aspen trees. So, what was wrong and why couldn't I shake this feeling of foreboding? Something was off.

I leaned back on the old metal bench and began to

people-watch while I waited for my latte. Maybe my blood sugar was just low. Whatever it was, I needed to shake it off. I heard the first band of the day as they started to tune up and folks were filling up the square and surrounding area. I watched as a businessman in a suit sauntered by with his briefcase. He seemed a little dressed up for this kind of event. A woman in a tight short skirt and heels stepped up to him. She latched onto his arm and planted a kiss on his cheek. They walked off arm in arm. I spotted two older ladies walking down one of the sidewalks across the town square. They looked like they were here for a day of shopping. I looked a little farther down the square and saw two men sitting on a bench. I couldn't help but wonder if they were the spouses of those two women. I laughed to myself and hoped that bench was comfortable, because they might be there for a while. I turned to see Maggie as she returned with two tall cups. There was a little curl of steam coming out of the lids.

"Here you go, my friend. Take a sip of this."

I took a careful sip. "Oh, that really is good. Pumpkin spice?"

"Yep," Maggie took a seat beside me on the bench.

"I have never been too much into pumpkin spice anything, but this is really good. I needed this." We sat there, sipped our lattes and watched as the activity in the square started to pick up. I closed my eyes, and tipped my head back, enjoying the sunshine and inhaling scents of BBQ that floated on the air. I could feel my shoulders relaxing. Maybe today would turn out okay after all. We sat on the bench, finished our coffee and enjoyed a moment of relaxation after our busy morning.

"Feel like an early lunch?" Maggie's voice interrupting my thoughts.

"Yes, but I promised Claudette that I'd check on her before lunch and see how she's doing at her booth." The Little Copper Cafe was officially closed today, but Claudette was selling some of her famous baked goods out on the square.

"Well let's go, I'm free to help."

We walked across the now-crowded town square. I looked around and spotted Claudette's booth. From the large group of customers around her booth it looked like she was doing a pretty good business. She looked up as we approached.

"Glad to see you ladies. Can you do me a favor?" she asked, after giving change back to a customer. Without waiting for a response from us, she said "Here're my keys, if you can please, run over to the cafe for me. I need some more scones, both the blueberry and the brown sugar cinnamon, some more orange cranberry bread and the blueberry muffins. They are already set out on the trays in the kitchen. You might have to make a couple of trips."

"Of course, we'll be right back." Maggie and I hurried off to the cafe and returned with the baked goods as requested. She had a lull in customers as we got back and we loaded up her booth.

"Thank you, ladies, I think that'll keep me for a while now. Why don't you go get some lunch and if you don't mind, come check on me later? I'd appreciate it."

"Happy too." I said to her.

"Sounds like a plan to me." Maggie tugged on my arm, "Come on Emily, lunch is calling my name."

I turned to follow Maggie, "Lead the way."

We wove our way through the crowds in the square, made it to Joe's and picked up some barbeque.

"How about that table over there, it has empty seats." I

nodded to a table under an oak tree on the edge of the square. I followed Maggie as she made her way over to the table, which was occupied by a couple. As I approached the table I could see the same gentleman I had seen earlier. The man wearing the suit and the lady that accompanied him.

"Are these seats taken?" Maggie asked before setting her plate down.

"No sugar, pull up a chair." The blonde lady had a heavy Southern drawl. She stood from her seat, giving the man a kiss on his almost bald head. "I'll go get your food and be right back, darlin'."

I set my food down on the table. "I'm going to go back and get me some tea; do you want some?" I asked Maggie.

"Yes, and can you manage a few more napkins too? Joe's barbecue sauce can get a little messy."

I wove my way back through the milling crowds again, picked up some napkins, our drinks then headed back to the table. I noticed the little blonde Southern belle as she walked a little ahead of me, carrying a tray.

"Oh honey, be careful! I sure don't want to spill something on you." The little Southern belle admonished a woman who had just bumped into her. Her Southern accent was thick and impossible to miss.

I watched as the dark-haired woman made her apologies and continued on her way. Wow, that was some black wig she was wearing. I watched her walk away, then chided myself; obviously there is a reason someone wears a wig. My gosh, when did I become so critical, I wondered as I rejoined Maggie at the table.

Maggie was holding a rib and licking the BBQ sauce off her fingers. "This barbecue is so good, and I love his green beans." She reached out to pluck a napkin from the top of the stack that I had just plunked down on the table.

I hadn't had anything from Joe's in a while; and today it seemed extra good. "I love his mashed potatoes. I never really thought about making them with parmesan cheese."

"You know, Joe took over the business from his father years ago. I don't think he has changed any of his recipes." Maggie commented in-between bites.

"With the way this food tastes, there wouldn't be any reason to change anything about it," I said reaching for another napkin.

"If you still feel hungry after you finish we could go back for cobbler." She was smiling wistfully.

"Ha! I love having friends who love to eat as much as I do."

"Larry, Larry, what's wrong?" We were interrupted by the sound of a Southern accent increasing in volume. She had brought back a plate of food and a drink for Mr. Suit man, who I just learned was named Larry, then gone off again to get her own food. She had just returned for the second time, putting her plate down on the table. I looked over and saw that she was bent down, her hands on the man's shoulders and her face filled with concern.

My attention turned to the man. I saw him gripping his stomach, his brow furrowed.

"I think it's starting again. I don't feel good at all. I think I need to go..."

He didn't even finish his sentence. He grimaced, clutching his stomach.

The Southern belle looked up at us, her eyes pleading for help, "Can you help me? I don't think I can get him up by myself."

The man groaned again and slumped over in his seat in my direction. It was all I could do to keep him from falling off his folding chair.

I turned to Maggie, and she was already dialing 911. Some men rushed over to provide their assistance, steadying him in his seat. An ambulance crew was there in just a few moments and loaded him up to take him to the community hospital. His wife, who was panic stricken, accompanied him. The scene caught the attention of almost everyone in the square. We were left wondering what in the world had just happened. Claudette came rushing over wanting to know the same thing.

"I don't know. We were just sitting here eating and he started to grip his abdomen. I hope he is alright. I feel bad for him and his wife. I knew something was going to happen today. I just had that feeling." I looked over at Claudette, "Do all of your town celebrations turn out like this?"

"My good heavens, no." Claudette responded.

The onlookers returned to what they were doing. I still felt a bit stunned at the turn of events.

"Are you two going to be okay?" Claudette asked. "I've got someone covering for me and I guess I should get back."

"Yes, go and we'll come check on you in a bit." I volunteered.

The rest of the day was uneventful and Maggie and I enjoyed browsing the booths, eating cobbler and listening to the music. Maggie was right, Dorothy Johnston's peanut butter fudge was the best I had ever eaten. For the most part my sense of dread had lifted, although there were still some random thoughts about Larry and his Southern belle. I really hoped he was going to be okay.

ABOUT THE AUTHOR

Hello readers.

My name is Amy and I'm the author of the Copper Ridge Mystery series. I'd like to say I've had a passion for writing my whole life, but that would be untrue. My husband of forty plus years encouraged me to try my hand at writing cozy mysteries in the spring of 2019 and I LOVE IT!

A former nurse, I live in the Houston area. I enjoy a quiet life with my husband, children, and grandchildren. My family also includes one lovable dog and five very independent cats. When I'm not writing I enjoy running marathons with support from my friends at Ft. Bend Fit, jigsaw puzzles and always a good cup of coffee.

I hope you will enjoy my Copper Ridge Mystery series and thank you for your support.

www.ingramcontent.com/pod-product-compliance
Lightning Source LLC
Chambersburg PA
CBHW020350130626
46549CB00006B/2251